Also by Ell

Novels

The Dump

Unbelievable Things

Walthamstow Central

Short Fiction

The Aleppo Button

Lenin's Trousers

To Wanstonia

Driving My Baby Back Home

Aria Fritta

Dead Iraqis: Selected Short Stories

(with Mac Daly) *Engels on Video*

Intolerable Tongues

Ellis Sharp

Zoilus Press

A Zoilus Press paperback
First published in Great Britain by Zoilus Press in 2011

A CIP catalogue record for this book is available from the British Library.

ISBN 978-1-902878-98-0

Typeset by Electrograd

Printed and bound by CPI Group (UK) Ltd, Croydon, CR0 4YY

To Keith Rowley

P

PURPOSE? HOW LONG do you intend to stay? Do you have a return ticket? These are questions you cannot escape. Sight-seeing, I retort, sweating. A journey of several weeks. Returning by way of Port Said. I dare not say: to write a book. That would be pride and presumption. Yet its absent presence foreshadows all that I'll do, all that follows. At the border everything is still as empty as the barren No Man's Land crossed since Ras en-Naqura. The future glimmers with the promise of the past. I am tense to tread in holy footsteps, they are close and everywhere. My greasy hand trembles at the thought of holding my pen, of putting it all down. All of it! *Jesus!* And I am a little shivery, too. I fell sick back there. A light fever still afflicts me, the official if curious he may not be he may be bored doubtless attributes my shining face to the heat. Back in the car I swallow another pill. In truth, I have been feverish since Tyre. No, be honest, since Cairo. Delete, rewrite. Let's get it straight. And true. For the lip of truth shall be established for ever: but a lying tongue is but for a moment. Perhaps it is the pills that have made me constipated. Or perhaps the climate. This heat is intolerable. It smothers me. Along the Acre Road misty purple beams quivered prettily upon the sea. The slow waves that break there are green and dark as upon any Hebridean shore. *Stringendo!* The barren jagged rocky coastline fell away, at once I was in Switzerland, on holiday (which means: Holy Day). Light-headed, in Zurich once, I prayed for release from sin. The glare from the white slopes intense, the car moving very slowly around curves treacherous as a pair of female breasts. Death was an enticing possibility – yet then, as now, I was not at the wheel. I was always a passenger, never a driver. Here I fly over the arid moon. It, too, is bright with our Lord's inaccessible scrutiny. I skim a blotchy waste, it is bright and uninhabited. And dirty. The Middle East is a very dirty place. In Geneva they would be appalled. The arid corrugated lunar soil matched in some way the ridges on my brow. Dust boiled behind us. I did not try to understand the metaphors which bubbled there. I let them cloudily burst. It's best to beware ripe adjectives. They can make you voluble. The French customs station assembles itself out of a barren residue, a few wearisome formalities, and then on towards the Mandate, the British wicket. Look! The Tegart Wall! Roll after roll of barbed wire, arranged around wooden trellising and spikes. An ingenious device to stop the flow of Arabs and arms. At intervals concrete blockhouses. Their symmetry is pleasing. Slits of blackness add to it. Inside those slits are invisible eyes and weaponry. British eyes, British weaponry. The thought thrills me. *Civis Romanus sum.* We pass through the wire to the checkpoint. Purpose, what is it? The unsmiling official is satisfied by my replies but he has words of warning. Do I understand that the situation is grave? It is Very Grave (he says with a grave expression). His Majesty's Government cannot be held responsible for anything that might befall me. I say yes, yes I understand, and he waves us on, it is three-twenty-five in the afternoon precisely, I shall put this in my book. *At three-twenty-five I crossed over into our Holy Land.* Here, the road seems rougher than in Syria, I took hold of the door grip, it is pointless to take unnecessary risks. I stared out of the window, I am on the brink of a matter of which I have long dreamed. I recognised this land. I had never set foot in it before and yet I had visited it many times.

Feverdreams. And Acre did not disappoint. I lit a cigarette and walked among its romantic mediaeval walls. A street vendor sold me a tiny Crusader's cross for my collection. As we completed the transaction forty Arab prisoners were led past, veils on head. They are from the military prison. Abbas tells me there are many, many rebels locked up here in cages. How many? I asked. He did not know. Hundreds, he said. An exaggeration, I assumed, but later, when I raised the matter with Monty, he told me there were 2,500 prisoners. Scum, he said. Bandits and gangsters the lot of them, he said. I leave my droll chauffeur by the car and climb the old fortifications. The view across the bay is astonishing. Haifa shines beyond a marge of palms. It is thirty-two minutes there by train, faster by car. There is a new macadam road, we are on the outskirts in no time. On the way we pass a peculiar sight: an Arab tied to the bonnet of the first lorry in an army convoy. I ask Abbas what this strange occurrence means but he does not hear me. On the edge of Haifa the huts of the pioneer Jewish colonists cluster on the sand wastes. A huge cement plant stands near the airport, electric power wires cross fields where long-horned cattle grazed, from behind a line of ancient palms rose storage tanks bearing the words **Iraq Petroleum**. Two buses pass by, going where Jesus went, NAZARETH-CANA-MAGDA is immediately followed by JERUSALEM-BETHLEHEM. Can there be a more fascinating or more important thing to know than the life and personality of a man from whose birth we date everything? What He did and said and was, and above all where. He grew up in the home of a working carpenter. Until He was about thirty he worked with His own hands at that craft. Then, for two or three years, He taught a group of young men, some of them fishermen. He healed people. He wrote no books. He had no army. He was never in any government. To get close to all that you have to follow the tracks He walked in Palestine. Could there be a drama more enthralling? A night at Haifa. I unpack and take out two books. One is the Bible, the other a detective story. Before lights out I read from both. I slept like the proverbial, rose early. The hotel had packed me a hamper. Abbas was waiting on time with the Rolls. Off we go!

A

ABBAS. YOU WOULD not expect an Arab to own a Rolls Royce but Abbas did. What model? I really have no idea. I care nothing for motor cars. The workings of the internal combustion engine are a complete mystery to a man such as myself. What lies beneath a bonnet is as obscure to me as the intestinal arrangements of a hippopotamus. There are certain things a man of the cloth needs to know and certain things he will never need to know. Suffice it to say that the Rolls was a big black brute. It had massive running boards, suitable for occasional use by servants. Its front portion was reminiscent of a gleaming sarcophagus. Abbas came highly recommended. He did motor tours and knew the region. Very reliable, they said in Cairo. Abbas won't let you down. I negotiated a divine pilgrimage. Abbas beamed. The deal was done. Friendly handshake! Haifa he knows well. The harbour bristles with activity at this hour. A Belgian freighter unloading iron roofing. Coils of wire from England to carry new electric light power. A crane landing bound frightened sheep. Commerce thrives now that the pipe line brings its oil from distant Iraq. On the outskirts construction work is going on under Moslem architects, Abbas takes the road heading east, motoring across the Plain of Esdraelon. Genesis 49 thuds in my head. A swelling rises beside the road, an ancient Canaanite fortress. Next the first in a series of police stations. Soon Megiddo itself, a pale mythic mound, purchased for the Oriental Institute, excavated by permission of the Palestine Department of Antiquities. Layer upon layer is being removed, entire strata. The layer which at present lies under the open sky is the Solomonic level. Breathlessly I ascend the narrow-gauge track down which tiny trucks bring out the glacis and unearthed specimens. The heat is intense. Thank goodness for my pith helmet, my enormous umbrella, purchased from Beirut bazaar, both extremely good value at the price. Although the helmet strap rubs. Here at Megiddo I rested in the shade of a wall. I watched the men and the women and the children as they toiled with their rubble. Be careful with that precious dust! And no slacking. For in all labour there is profit: but the talk of the lips tendeth only to penury. (Prov. Xiv. 23.) Megiddo is where King Solomon housed his cavalry. He had twelve thousand horsemen. He had fourteen hundred war chariots. It is all in the first Book of Kings. Sunlight shines once again on an exposed portion of twelve-foot wall. I am flung back in time, repeatedly. The excavations have exposed stalls for the horses, rooms for the grooms, parade grounds, storage silos and the outlines of massive structures. Elsewhere, at Gerar and Beth-pelet, the Petries found golden ear-rings, a collar of three strings of fine carnelian, black and white quartz, signs that the court of Solomon possessed jewellery much finer than the Egyptians of that era. Solomon was a merchant-king, a controller of trade routes. The Book of Kings tells us of his annual tributes from every man – gold, silver, garments, spices, horses, mules. At Megiddo there is more. The excavators are keen to get down to the levels indicated in chronicles, which tell of lapis lazuli, of a golden chariot and gorgeous vases. Heavy stone balls are strewn among the assorted débris. I pick one up to take home as a souvenir. As well as the catapult ball I took a vase handle. They will go nicely on my desk. Before going back down to Abbas, who is sitting on the running board of the car, picking his nose and scrutinising the dirt, I admire the view. I stand for some time, gazing at the fringe of trees on the distant hills of Nazareth. I think of Jesus and his childhood. There are some peculiar mediaeval tiles in the British Museum, I do not know what to make of them. They strike me as irreverent and unsuitable for public display. I wrote to the Director but he brushed my complaint aside. As did the Prime Minister. A fly pesters me and it is time to descend. I return to the car with a feeling of having enjoyed a satisfying meal of historical reality. Seven miles east of Megiddo is the site of Ta'anek fortress. Here the narrow track suddenly fills with a herd of fifty or more brown camels, driven along by ten or twelve Bedouin men and women and their shouting children. The wives wear trailing black gowns. A camel bares its teeth, resenting my Kodak. Soon they are gone, heading west to Armageddon. We are going east, to Beisan. We pass the collective farms of the busy, industrious Zionists. In the United States there are four Hachshare or preparation farms, where young Jews train. They are making a new world. They are doing the will of the Lord. This is their land, from time immemorial. Father taught me that. They say that when the Zionists break this ancient crust a foul miasma emerges from the fallow earth as it is ploughed for the first time. Continuing past the farms we come to the power lines of the Palestine Electric Corporation, whose poles parallel the road. Beyond the white building of the police station at Beit Alfa we come to Beisan's tiny station. The mound itself is huge. No sign of that threatened Emergency! I left Abbas at the car. He is an amusing fellow but not interested in history. Also he frets ceaselessly about his car (punctures, scratches, theft, troublesome urchins). I took the foot-trail leading upward. Here I sense the shades of the Philistines. Their hideous laughter crackles in my burning ears. I see them carry Saul's armour into the temple of the Ashtaroth. I see them fasten his head in the second Temple of Rameses, on this very height which I am now approaching. How time collapses beneath this heavy heat. The men of Jabesh and Gilead arose and went all night and took the body of Saul and the bodies of his sons from the wall of Beth-shan. And they came to Jabesh and burned them. And they took the bones and buried them under the tamarisk tree in Jabesh. I spot some yellowed bones in the excavated strata by the end of the steep little path to the summit. The skull indicates the remains of a sheep. Beisan was once called Scythopolis. Its population and commerce in the Roman era are said to have rivalled those of Jerusalem. Palestine was wealthy in Roman times. It yielded twelve million denarii in taxes. The Roman Government made it pay for its own conquest. It is the same to-day. Under the British Mandate the Palestine Government to-day has a surplus in its budget. How successfully England administers this complicated little land! And yet in all our hearts we know a deeper truth that drives such endeavour. *Whatsoever ye do, do it heartily, as to the Lord, and not unto men; knowing that of the Lord ye shall receive the reward of the inheritance: for ye serve the Lord Christ.* The estimated value of the salt, potash, bromine and magnesium chloride stored in the Dead Sea is about $1,182,000,000. Not to mention the revenues from the new Iraq Petroleum pipe line. Not to mention the millions of cases of oranges and grapefruit annually exported to England and elsewhere. Modern Palestine richly rewards its protectors. Abbas is busily dusting his magnificent vehicle. He drives me on to the acropolis of Beth-shan. Here the track is narrow and steep. The wheels spin on grit-coated slabs of rock. I close my eyes. The Rolls shakes and lurches. Camels and donkeys are a constant nuisance.

Sometimes I wish I had a pistol. A donkey is a stupid animal, though admittedly helpful to the poor. And, it goes without saying, to our Lord. My flesh shall rest in hope. For why? Thou shalt not leave my soul in hell. And at thy right hand there is pleasure for evermore. At long last we reach the gateway of the city. An Arab custodian in floating head-veil steps out, carrying a cane. He speaks not one word of English, other than the names Amenophis III and Rameses II. At least I think that is who he meant! His pronunciation left a lot to be desired. After that paltry effort he seemed to give up. He pointed his cane at the ground, jabbering in Arabic. It is fortunate that I have genned up on this place. Oh yes, I have done my reading. My McEwan Blue Guide is a boon. It educates me about the symmetries. I know I am looking at the ground-plan of the great temple complex which belonged to the god Makal. Column bases and broken masonry lie all about. A sharp cold gust blows through the ruins. It agitates the dust. Jesus must often have passed by this way. Out of this citadel mound steps an Englishwoman. She says her name is Muriel. Another pilgrim. She is from Basildon. I offer her a ride but she stiffly declines. She is not yet finished with her investigations. Her tone is not particularly warm. Suspicious, even. Surely she cannot believe I have carnal intent. I explained I was from the Outer Hebrides. She sniffed. She had been to Scotland once, many years ago. She had not enjoyed the experience. I mention The Emergency. Is she not worried about her safety? Another sniff. Her stockings are aptly blue, her hair a lurid black. She bobs back into the ruins. Good riddance! No, that was unkind. I take it back. For God resisteth the proud, but giveth grace unto the humble. The truth is the heat is making me fray a little at the edges. And the guide is beginning to irritate me. He deposits numerous explanations upon me, which I neither require nor understand. Then he has the impertinence to expect a tip! All Arabs are the same. They are like parasites, feeding off their host. I clenched my fist and waved it and curtly told the fellow to leave me alone, which he finally did, retreating with angry mutters into a little wooden hut, as an insect might hide under a stone. I am glad to be gone from that place. The citadel mound dustily recedes. Abbas parked in the little modern village of Beisan and went off to buy himself food. I stayed in the car and ate a delicious picnic luncheon packed by my hotelier in Haifa. The natives tentatively emerge from their homes. They approach, smiling. I feed them caramels. This makes them happy. Palestinians adore caramels. I distribute them plentifully in the days and weeks that follow.

VERY OCCASIONALLY I contribute verses to church magazines, and it is quite widely recognised that I have something of a gift. It has even been suggested that I collect my contributions into a single volume, for both the cultural and spiritual benefit of mankind. This would be a detestable vanity, and I am content for my modest addition to the wonders contained in *The Golden Treasury* of Master Palgrave to be assessed posthumously! Yet I cannot, must not, entirely conceal the impact which Capernaum in Galilee made upon me.

It's sunrise out in Galilee, where mists of Moab melt
Before the dawn's new ecstasy on seas His feet have felt.
With sunrise also in my heart I stand here looking down
Where our dear Lord's own hand once touched folk in this town.
The Son of Righteousness has come, with healing in His wings,

While in the market there's a hum, and my heart swells
and sings.

Did even Keats ever quite equal such lines as these? But out with thee, detestable pride! A man must not boast of his gifts, to the detriment of the less talented, the less fortunate. Christian principle forbids the sweet enticements of vanity. Let them acclaim my genius after death, for today I am set on Higher Things. Today Tiberias helps visualise what Capernaum looked like when it teemed with a busy population, crowding the shores of the Lake. Little boats ride at anchor as if about to 'put out into the deep.' The opposite hills of Gilead are draped in morning mist (rhymes with 'kissed'!). But sadly Tiberias today smacks too much of Herodian luxury, for, alas, it has a 'Lido Beach' and a 'dance pavilion.' So quickly on, to the ruins of Capernaum, to seek the footprints of Christ in His spiritual 'H.Q.' – a place where He enjoyed His happiest days of fruitful ministry. Ah, the joys of Galilee. Here He was appreciated as He never was in Nazareth. Here He was loved. Here He was thronged. Here He toiled. Here He relaxed. Here He 'spake many things.' The Sea of Galilee is magical at twilight. As one gets nearer its waters one knows not whether to sing for joy or weep for very stirring of His life within. I was suddenly irritated to see that Abbas had lit a cigarette. I rapped on the glass and shouted at him to stop. For a while he pretended not to hear, then in the end sullenly removed it from his lips and tossed it out of the window. This was reckless of him. It might well have resulted in a conflagration. But the Arab is a creature of impulse and can sometimes be difficult to tame. The Sea of Galilee is six-hundred-and-eighty feet below sea level. This heart-shaped lake is exalted to the heavens for its gracious ministry to Christ. To have it ruined by a cigarette and a morose chauffeur was loathsome. Abbas accelerated and started taking the bends too fast. Once again I had to bang on the glass and remonstrate. The wretch became even dourer. I swivelled my gaze and tried to forget he existed. To sweep along the shores of Galilee's turquoise lake is an other-worldly experience. It is 'such stuff as dreams are made of.' The scene should really be felt rather than described. The late hour throws a golden radiance onto the opposite hills. They look kneaded and worked down and baked brown by ages of sun and wind. Then, without warning, they become a golden amethyst. I felt them cast over me a spell of invitation, just as they did to the weary Jesus. What urgings they put upon Him! Come over unto the other side, they gently whispered. I remembered at that moment to put some cream upon my cheeks, to prevent damage. The birthplace of Christianity can at times be cruel to those who nowadays are best placed to preserve and spread its glories! Along the shoreline whitecaps break over piles of stones. These ever-thinning rocks and pebbles are the eloquent remnants of the cities Jesus knew – their piers, their shops, their houses. Matthew, the tax-collector of Capernaum, walked in their midst. Here trod the feet of busy Peter and his partner Andrew. These stones cry out their stories to those of us with understanding hearts. At Tel Hûm we halted. I left Abbas sulking in his glass cage and explored the open-air museum. What a fascinating collection of oil presses and meal-mills the German friars have accumulated here! There are also the capitals of ancient fluted columns and restored portions of a Roman synagogue. A black-edged sombre notice states that the superintending Franciscan Father paid for it with his life, through a snake bite. Tear-bottle recesses; bas reliefs of Jewish emblems, such as the five-pointed star; Roman chariot wheels. An accumulated encrustation of Graeco-Roman faith. What rivets my attention are the floor mosaics, from a hexagonal fore-court by the shore. The waves of Galilee spray a rainbow mist. This may well be a floor which Jesus walked. The stones themselves seem to whisper it. I feel His immanence in this place, lit by the glorifying light of the sunset. I see before me the glowing outline of the divine feet. I can actually hear the music of His voice. Oddly, it has a faint Glaswegian accent. There is a strange clarity to this moment. I seem to be surrounded by a luminous multitude. Their faces are rapt with wonder. The speaker smoothes His beard and addresses them calmly. I have not found so great faith, He says. No, not in all Israel. The crowd sighs. No more complimentary word was ever spoken by Jesus. A cloud passes over the sun and the illusion is broken. A moment later the golden flood returns, but not the ghosts of yesteryear. The imprints of His two feet fade. Suddenly, like Peter, I feel like getting wet. So, shoes off! Onto the blue-green stones I step. Ankle-deep in opal water I tread Christ's Capernaum. I might almost be in a 'movie'. Wave after burnished wave breaks musically upon this eloquent strand. This is Galilee's heart-beat. The sun like a giant ruby slips away and the whole landscape reddens. The Lake takes on an emerald tint. I picture Him here. He walks the market-places at that evening hour when orientals come alive. He is summoned to the bedside of the mother of Peter's wife. I hear Peter calling men to follow His growing group. As day ends and Capernaum turns to amethyst I see Him. He lays His hand on the swarming groups of little boys at play among the boats. I prod lazybones Abbas awake and he takes me on to Tabgha, which is probably Bethsaida. Here are rare mosaics of the early Christian church. Loaves and fishes in the design attest the belief that here the miraculous feeding took place. This is a likely thing, since the place is called Heptapegon. That means Seven Springs. The mosaics are in charge of a barefooted Bedouin. She wears a long black dress, touched with embroideries of red. Getting down on her hands and knees, she scrapes off the covering of sand and dirt. This is the only protection these mosaics have, as they lie in the open. In a spirit of Christian fellowship I kneeled alongside her, using one of her shoes to scoop away the sand. I regret to say she responded with incoherent invectives. I endeavoured to forgive her somewhat coarse, possessive manner. Moslem though she is, Jesus is her prophet. Since these mosaics have something to do with Him, she must jealously guard them. I stood back and left it to her. Abbas, who had sauntered over, had an unpleasant smirk on his face. A fly began to bother me. I sent a splinter of prayer, asking that it pester Abbas instead. To my delight it did! The exposed mosaics are of amazing interest. The early-Christian symbols are dazzling. Very clear loaves and fishes. Ducks, and some life-like geese. A crane carrying a snake in its mouth. Thistles! A round tower. Some Greek letters spelling out the glory of God's name. My McEwan's tells me these are fifth century. Abbas took me back to Tiberias. I dined at a very clean German hotel there. The Fuehrer may not be everyone's cup of tea but there is something deeply impressive about the German concern for order and hygiene. This is not to deny the shadow cast by 'the Jewish question.' But even this can be horribly exaggerated by irresponsible newspaper men. I do not myself believe that Herr Hitler had anything at all to do with the excesses which have reportedly been committed on his behalf. It is also noteworthy that the German Zionist Federation has deplored emotive attempts at a boycott of German goods. This kind of nonsense is inspired by communists and socialists for their own sinister purposes. The German government has, quite rightly in my view, cracked down hard on 'trades unionists' and the miscellaneous rabble of the so-called 'Left'. But I digress. I saw that the Lake surface was now disturbed. The boom surged against the shore. I could easily picture the anxious disciples tossed in their little craft, alarmed even though Christ was aboard. At the hotel I had arranged to be taken out on the Lake. A blond German introduced me to Najim, who lived locally. He was a handsome young man with an engaging smile. Abbas grunted at the intruder, and retreated inside the Rolls. Najim had brought a torch. He guided me down the dark, narrow, uneven street which led to the wharf. This was not far from a white building bearing in large blue capitals words which brought a surge of patriotic feeling into my breast: SCOTTISH MEDICAL MISSION. Outside it a number of natives squatted on the steps, smoking hubble-bubble pipes. Strangely, they owned a small portable gramophone. From the crackly speaker came the unexpected tinkling of ragtime. These men ignored me completely. I might almost have been as invisible as the hero of Mr Wells's tale. Along the dock there were a number of prone figures, laid out like corpses. They turned out to be boatmen, asleep. Najim explained that several of the boats were scheduled to leave at 4 a.m. He led me down a steep flight of steps. A substantial fishing boat bobbed up and down in the night waters. There were seven others already seated there. They were fellow Christian pilgrims like myself. Three American couples and a sombre Norwegian. We sat at one end, the sturdy oarsmen at the other. Soon we had pulled away from the quayside and were out into the calm waters. Above us blazed the stars and constellations that Christ Himself saw from this very place. Orion, the Pleiades, the

Pole Star of the Mariner. The Great Dipper looked near enough to bring down and drink from its shimmering silver. One of the American women drew from her case a trumpet and began to blow All Through the Night. She followed this with Jesus, Saviour, Pilot Me. We sang along. Silent Night was followed by Abide With Me. Then, with trumpet muted to the slenderest filament of sound, she led us into Perfect Day. It made me think of that day two thousand years before when He said, Let us go over unto the other side. And there arose a great storm of wind. And the waves beat into the boat, insomuch that the boat was now filling. And our Lord lay in the stern, asleep on the cushion. And they prodded Him and said unto Him, Teacher, carest not thou that we perish? And He awoke, and rebuked the wind, and said unto the sea, Peace, be still. And the wind ceased, and there was a great calm. Hasn't this been the most heavenly day you have ever lived? one of the American women says on the way back. We all feel elated. Our faith has been recharged. If only we could have brought all the atheists of the world with us. This reality would have melted them utterly. One cannot doubt Him in Galilee. It just won't let you. The exhilaration of an evening like this makes sleep a waste of time. I just want to go on and on, experiencing Him I want to look for the print of His feet on these shores that he loved. Two in the morning. A great company of cocks begins crowing. Nowhere in the world is the crow of a cock so strident as in Palestine. I remembered the hour of Peter's denial. Here Christ Jesus chose a telling bit of local colour. From my hotel room I can hear the soft feet of camels going by my window. They jingle their way toward Nazareth. I cannot describe, I cannot explain, the thrill I get from a camel train, a camel train with burdens and bumps and beads and bells and wobbly humps. It comes from the markets of old

Bagdad with rugs and silks I should like to have had. A camel train on thistles fed, yet walking along with a regal tread. By five the vague stirrings of native life begin. In the Galilean household below a mother rolls up the mat on which she has been sleeping. She places it on her husband's bed. A baby's cradle of bright wool swings from a crude framework to which rush matting is attached. There is no other furniture. A child departs with a five-gallon tin. The woman's husband resembles Abbas. He is still asleep. The baby tries to pull him awake. The mother brings flat cakes of coarse bread for breakfast. How I would like to fly down like an angel! I would startle them with offerings of caramels. One, too, for the man beneath my window. He walks by carrying to market one puny little chicken. The sun still not yet up. The natives understand the importance of getting going before dawn. Later the heat will become intense. It pours into this sub-sea-level locale like lava. The bays burn deep and chafe. Across the Lake I see the misty hills of Gilead. From under black and grey opalescent clouds hanging low against the page I see the sun shoot out spectacular rays of adjectives onto a blank-blank sea. My mind's diseased, this much is obvious. A half hour away, up in the hills of Galilee, lies the Mount itself. On and up! The burning Plains of Hattin suck me into the boiling heart of the Mount of Beatitudes. Whoever shall compel thee to go one mile, go with him two. A moral which sometimes made poor Abbas a little sulky! As we ascended I began to sing O Master, Let Me Walk With Thee. Mister Grumpy responded by stepping on the gas. Once more I had to admonish the oaf. I told him finally to stop. I wandered among the thorns and stones. Above me I saw a little hill. Here truly are the imprints of Christ. Not in the sun-baked ground that my feet are treading but in my heart, where His truths are implanted. Blessed are they that hunger after righteousness. The pilgrim-presence of the Teacher overwhelmed me with His love. Light swirled around me. The whole of the area at the base of the Sea of Galilee is a mass of golden flowers, shoulder high. Elsewhere there are delphiniums and stocks and tulips. There are poppies, hyacinths, marigolds and hollyhocks. The impact of this lively expedition upon my constipation was, I regret to say, nil.

ANOTHER PILL. THERE, swallowed! Still in a fever, you see…

A SON OF the manse is one way of describing me, I shall not object. The house was built of dark grey stone and contained many empty rooms. I was born there, grew up there, and still live there. I was nourished on the milk of the Word. Winter was caustic. Hebridean gales are powerful and loud. I could hear the trees screaming. No room was ever warmed. Father did not believe in heating. Heating belonged to the Devil, who wanted to soften sinners for his realm. I sat in my overcoat, hands clasped around my neck for warmth. On Sundays we dressed in black and ate stewed mutton shanks. At four years old I had the words of Onward, Christian Soldiers. Bread and dripping was an afternoon treat. Sometimes a pear. Father spoke often of the utter impossibility of anyone on whom sin is seen by the eye of divine justice ever escaping God's righteous sentence of death by any effort to justify himself. He spoke of it frequently. And the word utter he uttered very emphatically. The brilliance of his stare was stark. His eyeballs swelled and the lids became animated, as might one suffering from blepharospasm. In the last days perilous times shall come. There shall be: Trucebreakers, Boasters, Blasphemers, Despisers of those that are good.

There shall be: Scoffers saying, Where is the promise of His coming? All things continue as they were. I sang hymns as loudly as I could and did not attempt to wriggle out of the divine vengeance that was my lot. Death lapped the house in many guises. Worms ate the mouldy apple tree and its lecherous pink-cheeked fruits. Crows cawed with laughter at the purgatory in store for me. The seething innards of a dead sheep were put there to instruct me in the weakness of the flesh. The touring sexton, Mr Feeder, scowled down at me. His narrow eyes saw every inch of my badness. The yew groaned for release from all things mortal. A poplar blew over one night. Its terrific crash pierced my soul. God was sending me many warnings. I was frail and vulnerable. I must eat my porridge and be a good boy. I must pray repeatedly for forgiveness for my heap of sins. Envy, gluttony, frivolity, laziness. Lust was not yet in the pile. Later, in my early teens, two books were always waiting for me when I returned home from the hills. By then I had lust well under my belt. How hot and bloated I was with sin in those lusty years! My cheeks burned brightly, my bony chest was cool with the sweat of my grubby endeavours. What a boisterous boy I was at fourteen! Sometimes I bruised myself in my ardent sinning. Sometimes those filthy impulses made my chest raw. I climbed trees and pressed myself close to the trunk. There I shuddered, my legs clamped as to a lover's back. Afterwards, besmeared and harrowed, I descended. Out there in the wilderness the bracken brushed my ankles. It was like a tiny barbed prelude to all the greater punishments to come. I shed drops of blood when my skin was slashed. I bled into my grey socks. A woman came from the village to do our washing. Her name was Nora. She resembled a crag. The Lord informed her duties. Nora was a spinster. I doubt that the stains on my bedding or the grey flakes on my handkerchiefs meant anything to her. If they did she would have been too inhibited to mention it to my father. Satan was abroad but his foul influence was not associated with obscure deposits on cotton. One book was the Holy Bible, the other was an atlas of the Holy Land. They were twins. How alive the stories came when I located them on a map! Judea, Samaria, Galilee. Decapolis. The regions were differently coloured in pale shades. Samaria was violet. Olive green flooded Decapolis. Galilee was turquoise, Judea flesh-coloured. The names were exotic and magical. They dripped a strange poetry. Each place had a narrative to its name. Jericho, Beersheba, Jerusalem. Bethlehem, Gaza, Nazareth. The Salt Sea. The Sea of Galilee. And all still there, nineteen centuries after His feet had passed that way. One day, Donald, you will go there. That was what father said. He would have gone himself but he was anxious about his chest. He coughed a lot. I won't make old bones, he'd say. It was quite a favourite expression of his. His outlook was generally morose. The news made him shake his head. Satan's influence was everywhere. The evil one was behind all the wars and revolutions and unrest. Satan had invented the doctrines of socialism and communism to pervert men's minds and make them dissatisfied with their lot. Religion was under threat as never before. Fallen, fallen is Babylon the great, which hath made all the nations to drink of the wine of the wrath of her fornication. Fornication! A word which my father never explained. His big fat red dictionary said it meant Sexual intercourse between unmarried persons. But that did not clarify matters. Intercourse was talking and sexual talking was as clear as mud and anyway sexual was itself enigmatic, naughty, unspeakable. Instinctively one knew the boundaries. And fornication remains a word which still inspires dread. In my twenties the only woman who I ever dared to think I might marry was Mary Appleby, who taught Bible studies. Her disposition was cheerful, her breasts very substantial. She used talc a lot, judging by her pleasant odour. I enjoyed talking to her, though I flushed a lot, thinking of a side to my character of which she was innocent. I intimated the pleasures of a domestic arrangement and she did not demur. She was a woman I could have folded in two. When it came to the crunch, in Zurich, the thought of intercourse was awful. It would have tied us into a knot. We had a kind of unofficial engagement and then I called it off. Mary wept but I knew it was for the best. Perhaps I am not giving the whole story but it is at best, like Edwin Drood's, an incomplete tale. Yet in this vale of tears, and even when gales tore down our fencing, and sheep escaped from their pens, there was a ray of hope in a world rotten with sin. For the Jews are God's chosen people. Did not the Lord make a covenant with Abraham? *And I will give unto thee, and to thy seed after thee, the land wherein thou art a stranger, all the land of Canaan for an everlasting possession; and I will be their God.* Let no man deny the truths of Genesis. Eretz Israel. A land barren for twenty-hundred stony years. A land without people for a people without a land. A place in which to build a community which will be a bridge into the East. It will bear the culture and the sympathies of every great nation in its bosom. Let there be a great migration! Let the torch of visible community be lit! Let Israel be a nation of many nations! Let it provide a hearth for the Jewish spirit to manifest itself in a new order! A Jewish National Home in Palestine! These were my father's heated and thudding certainties and so, too, are they mine. All the more so now that I am here, in boiling Palestine, hearing the grasshoppers chant their litanies amid the olive groves. I palpitate in this astonishing heat. It is sticky as treacle, thick as towelling. My helmet is a great boon. Also my expensive horn-rimmed American sunglasses with the Crooks lens. Also my box of soaps.

THROUGH THE WILDERNESS of Ziph I zip. I zig-zag, hot in pursuit of Elijah! My father reminds me more of Elijah than anyone. Elijah was a big, lean, vigorous man, unafraid to challenge Baal. A man prepared to do combat with Queen Jezebel and a deluded people. They called Elijah a troubler of the people but he retorted that they worshipped false gods. Elijah asserted the primacy of Yahweh, and proved it with the aid of the four elements. In victory he had the prophets of Baal put to death. Elijah traversed all the extremities of our Holy Land. He trekked restlessly on errands of perpetual protest against a soft civilisation and the false worship which made it putrefy. The western seaboard, the southern deserts, all this he knew. He later went east. He vanished from sight in Gilead. The marvel is that all Elijah's landmarks may be visited by the motor-pilgrim to-day. There is the added bonus of rewarding and picturesque scenes from native life along the way. One of the great dramas in the life of Elijah followed his victory over the priests of Baal. A messenger arrived to warn Elijah that Baal-worshipping Jezebel had vowed to take his life that very day. Assassins were on their way. Our prophet took to his heels. He came to Beersheba, which belongeth to Judah. I am headed there myself. I rose very early. By five-thirty my chauffeur had me on the excellent road south to Bethlehem. By six-thirty we were in Hebron. Here flat-roofed houses and domed buildings cling to the sides of hills, with Moslems concentrated in the old city near the Mosque. A friendly Arab from the American Mission School shows me Joseph's Tomb, Abner's Grave and Sarah's Spring. I longed to visit the ancient glass furnaces for the sake of their matchless blue products. But a hot sun calls to hasten. By seven we are on our way east toward the Desert of Beersheba. Here, men plough the last arable land with a crooked stick, just as in antiquity. From Tell es Zif you can get glimpses of the Mediterranean. Footpaths criss-cross the barren, cave-pocked hills. Paradise for a fugitive like Elijah. On, and we meet a settlement of black Bedouin tents, pitched by wealthy nomads on their way to Bagdad. They are descendants of Ishmael. Noon now, and I sip Arab coffee made in a tiny brass pot. I eat dry *durra* bread and gulp down a draught of cool water from an earthen jug. It is all the Arabs here have but they offer to share it. All the aspects of desert life which Elijah saw can still be seen today. Camels, donkeys, women mending the rips in the tents. Not far away there's a relic of Roman times – the golden arches of an aqueduct, looking as if it was built but only yesterday. And then the first green trees of Beersheba oasis. The wells here may have been sunk by Abraham. Genesis seems as fresh as that aqueduct. And Abraham planted a tamarisk tree in Beersheba… A bearded Arab fills his goatskin bag from a well. Possession of these ageless springs was essential to Allenby's strategy. His army took control in October 1917. Beersheba town contains a substantial mosque, a tiny hospital, a government building, a Traveller's Rest House, Allenby Square and a War Cemetery. Under some dying trees I stared at the bust of Lord Allenby. From Beersheba, Elijah continued on alone into the wilderness. Finally he sat down under a juniper tree and fell asleep. He woke to the touch of an angel. Bread and a flagon of water were at his side. The angel instructed him to partake of this refreshment. Elijah did so and once more fell asleep. A second time the angel woke him. Again he was told to eat and drink what had been provided, for he had a long journey ahead of him. And when all these holy adventures were over, horses and chariots of fire were in attendance. At the end a whirlwind lifted Elijah to heaven. Beyond Beersheba is a lonely waste of low hills, untenanted except by wandering Bedouin. Abbas drove me some miles into to it to get the feel of the place for my book. One mound attracted my attention. On its summit stood a solitary, motionless horseman. Against the intense sky he resembled a statue. And then over the crest came camels, hundreds of them. I had never seen so many in my life. Abbas braked and the beasts came lumbering by. Some brushed the sides of the car and Abbas shouted angrily and clapped his hands. This had no effect whatever. The horseman came down to us. He was a fierce-looking individual. He had a cartridge belt around his waist and a Damascene dagger tucked into his belt. He spoke a few words to Abbas, spat (evidently in contempt) and rode away. More camels bumped the car but this time Abbas said nothing. A new distraction quickly presented itself. A heavily veiled woman walked by, barefoot, yet evincing an indescribable hauter. Abbas leapt out and called after her. Whatever he said did not make the woman respond. She coolly walked on. Abbas turned to me and said, Amber, boss! Then he ran off. He caught up with her and walked alongside, jabbering in persuasive Arabic. It was her amber necklace he wanted. But it was not for sale. Sweat dripped from Abbas's cheeks as he beseeched her to part with this adornment. Instead of replying she mounted a donkey. She rode off at the head of a flock of black goats. As she rode away she drew from her garment a distaff, on which she spins wool as she jogs along. She is as incredible as the Duchess in *Alice in Wonderland.*

L

LATER ON DURING our adventures we slowed for an obstruction. We were in the district the Romans called Sabastia. Jesus passed this way from Nazareth to Jerusalem on a number of occasions. The land here is lush and fertile. Carobs and olives. Expanses of golden wheat. A distant crackling, as of gunfire. My head, perhaps. It rocks with fierce thoughts and little wandering points of piercing pain. Time for another pill. My temple burns and drips. I rise above my petty sufferings. My mouth waters at the thought of figs and dates. Olives however I have never particularly liked. To my olfactory sensitivities there's a tang of urine. Look! Up ahead, barrels have been placed across the road. As we drew close I saw that they were arranged in such a way as to require a vehicle to move around them in slow zig-zags. This is The Emergency. Beyond the barrels I saw a line of British army lorries. Troops milled around beside them. A soldier with a rifle stood between the first two barrels, holding up an arm. Abbas stopped the car. I wound down my window and stuck my head out. The soldier ignored Abbas and came over to me. I'm sorry, sir. You can't come through here today. The soldier turned to Abbas. You have to turn round and go back, you understand? Abbas nodded. But a second figure had appeared. An officer. His scrutiny absorbed my collar. I say, are you a vicar? I am a church minister, yes. Look, perhaps you could do me a favour. The fact is our Padre is away in Cairo and we don't have anyone. To look after the spiritual, I mean. What I really mean to say is that we've had a bit of trouble in these parts.

We gave the blighters quite a pasting but the swine managed to shoot one of our chaps. The doc reckons he's at death's door. If you could come and have a few words with him it might make all the difference. Forgive him his sins and all that. It can cheer a chap up no end when he's on the way out. I know I'd want it. Think you could manage it? I would be delighted. The officer jumped on to the running board and held on. He slapped the roof as one might the flanks of a horse. Abbas got the message and we rolled on, weaving our way around the barrels. The troops stopped chatting and stared. Soon we had left them behind. We came to another roadblock, a wooden contraption supporting coils of barbed wire. The officer waved at the soldiers and they dragged their barricade aside to let us through. We came to a town in a low valley. It was filled with activity. Something had torn a path through the middle of these dwellings. It was as if a great flood of water had gouged out a path. There was rubble everywhere. Some of the houses stood with just one side missing, exposing their interiors. Incredibly, some of these structures still contained people. Families moved around inside. I looked more closely: the occupants were all women and children. Many were weeping. Some of the women were making a terrible din, howling and banging their fists on the ground. We'll have to walk from here, the officer said. Abbas stayed with the car. The officer had a slim intelligent face, a sharp nose, a trim moustache. I could see soldiers smashing up furniture with their rifle butts and tipping jars of olive oil over rugs and cushions. In one living room stood a cabinet filled with glassware; an officer opened a door and dragged the structure forwards, stepping aside as it crashed across the carpet. Everyone paused at the sudden, sharp sound of shattering glass, then saw what it was and returned to their work of destruction.

A trooper with a pick helve was energetically breaking a set of wooden chairs. Another was setting fire to a large book, which I guessed was the Koran. A clock was stamped on, a mirror broken. Sacks of flour, wheat, rice and sugar were being emptied into a single pile. Then a soldier who looked about eighteen urinated into it, to the laughter of his fellow soldiers. Is that really necessary? I said. My escort said: absolutely. This place is a rebel stronghold. They deserve everything they get. The bandits put up stiff resistance to our boys so you can't expect them not to be angry. It was hellish, trying to get the wogs in this rabbit's warren of buildings and narrow alleyways. Too many enfilading fields of fire. He smiled. So we got the sappers in. That resolved that little difficulty. I take it you have never heard of Thomas Bugeaud? I had not. *La Guerre des Rues et des Maisons* is an inspiration. The Marshall shows how a detonator always has an advantage over the man in the street. A mob is blocking it with barricades? No matter. One goes indoors and passes it by systematically blasting through the walls of the houses. This works for us where snipers are concerned. If they try and trap us in a labyrinth of alleyways, the solution is simple. He laughed. He said emphatically: Remove the labyrinth. He laughed louder. We walked by a house with its door open. I glimpsed a trail of dried blood across the hallway. A couple of spent cartridges winked like little nuggets of gold. Soldiers sat around in the shade, having a rest. I was wondering where the men from this township were. This conundrum was soon solved. We came to a square where a hundred or so Arabs were held in a makeshift pen. They were guarded by troops with rifles. A scruffy-looking officer with a beard was sat behind a trestle table. Evidently he was interrogating the prisoners, one by one. Some were released, others detained. Over here, reverend. My escort impatiently called me over to a house further up the street. We went inside. A pair of troopers were standing by a shape on the ground. A lad lay on a rug, his head pillowed by a purple cushion. A sheet draped him from the waist down. The area around the crotch was scarlet and wet. The soldier looked no older than seventeen. His flawless skin was the colour of oatmeal. His lips were oddly colourless. His eyes stared dully upward. We were in someone's home but there was no one around. The soldier had been laid in a kind of ante-room. It was bare apart from a large Ali Baba vase. The officer whispered in my ear. The doctor says he's on the way out. So we'll leave you to it, vicar. He indicated to the two guards that they should remove themselves. He followed them out, closing the door. The sunlight went too. The room dimmed. It was cool and shadowy in there. The soldier suddenly reached out and grabbed my hand. Mother, he said. My child, I replied. I laid my free palm on his brow. It was cold with death. His spirit was departing. An odd memory came into my mind. Once, somewhere deep in childhood, I had witnessed the draining of an ornamental lake. I cannot imagine where it was. There was a sluice, and big men with cloth caps, and my father seemed to know the other adults. I stared as the water sank lower and lower. At the end of it there was a morass of black filth. A few puddles remained. These dark stinking pools were turbulent with motion. They contained eels. The eels seemed gigantic. They were like serpents in the illustrations in my boy's adventure books. The eels thrashed around, appalled at losing most of what made up their world. They feared the future. They wriggled and jumped, hoping to find a route back into the past. But already men with waders were making their way through the sludge. They carried staves. I was invited to partake of the flesh of the serpent. It tasted salty and sour and I spat it out. The cloth-capped men laughed. That day has always made me fearful of swimming. You never know what lurks beneath even the most tranquil surface. Pikes. Or as in that fearful Sherlock Holmes story, a hideous jellyfish. A lovely day at Chanctonbury Ring, the lad said. His eyes were open now. His irises were grey. His eyelashes were long and delicate as a girl's. Palestine does strange things to men's hair. The Jews with peculiar curls of hair fixed against their brows, for example. An officer with a beard, for example. The soldier fixed his gaze on me, but I am sure it was not me he was seeing. I remember the primroses, he said. I remember the hillside. You painted the hard boiled eggs, mother. You put faces on them. And flowers. We rolled them down the slope. The eggs cracked. We had a lovely picnic. While he burbled softly a door to my right abruptly opened. A man stood there. He was a bearded Arab, with wild eyes and a weatherbeaten, wrinkled face. He carried a rifle, which he pointed at me. His gaze took in the dying soldier, the bloodied sheet, my dog collar. I wondered if I should offer him a caramel. But the opportunity never arose. Our encounter was over in a jiffy. He put his finger to his lips, smiled, and quietly closed the door again. It was a very odd thing to have happened. It was some moments before it occurred to me that he must have been one of the rebels. But there was nothing I could do. My duty was to attend to the unfortunate in front of me. It was a dreadfully close shave, yet at the time I seemed to be in a sort of trance. Oddly, I felt no fear. The lad was still reminiscing. He said there were sixty wogs. They'd surrendered. They walked along the valley, hands held high. And then we machine-gunned them. All sixty. The Ulsters and West Kents did this. Most of the dead were boys. Most not even as old as me. Father will I go to hell? No, my son. Paradise is the place for you. The Lord forgives all.

I glanced at my watch, wondering how much longer he would continue. I had to get on. Jericho had to be fitted in. I decided not to beat about the bush. Now the soldier was talking about the beach at Hove. He was talking about sandcastles. I put both my hands around his and applied some gentle pressure. I am the resurrection and the life, saith the Lord, I said. He that believeth in me, though he were dead, yet shall he live: and whosoever liveth and believeth in me shall never die. That got his attention. He stopped his drift and gazed at me, a slight bewilderment on his face. Mother had probably never said this kind of thing to him. I know that my redeemer liveth, and that he shall stand at the latter day upon the earth. And though after my skin worms destroy this body, yet in my flesh shall I see God. Worms, he said. I don't like worms. We brought nothing into this world, and it is certain we can carry nothing away. Nothing away, he echoed. His eyes wandered around the walls, as if seeking something. His general demeanour reminded me somewhat of that of a drunkard. I noticed for the first time what looked like the nest of something, built into a dark, high corner. It was about the size of a cricket ball, but with a scaly coating. I don't think the soldier noticed it. His gaze returned to my face. Who in hell are you? he remarked, frowning. And then his head lolled forwards and I knew he was dead. It occurred to me that the officer had not even told me his name. I felt for his pulse. It seemed not to exist. I went outside and found the officer smoking a cigarette. He's dead, I said. I did what I could. In fact I think my presence perked him up, although to be honest he wasn't quite altogether there. I gave him the Lord's blessing. He talked about his mother a lot. They often do, the officer said. He pulled out a notebook. Could you give me his dying words? He nodded at his pad. He grinned nervously and bared his nicotine-stained teeth. A front molar was missing. I have to write to the parentals, he explained. They like to know what happened. He spoke with great affection of both his mother and father, I lied (forgive me O Lord). His mother especially. He said he hoped to meet them both again in heaven. Splendid. That's just the ticket. They'll like that. Oh and by the way, there's one of your bandits in the house. Good God! Why on earth didn't you say so? I have just said so. Yes, I suppose you have. That's true. I described what had happened. The officer narrowed his eyes, as they do in films. He called out to the pair of soldiers huddled nearby in the shade. Gregson – go and tell Sergeant Smith I need his unit over here at the double. Manning – go and find a stretcher and someone to help remove Moorehouse. He's snuffed it. The men went off. I'd better be getting back to my car, I said. We've another forty miles to go today. At least. Not this way, I'm afraid. Too jolly risky. Most of the rebels fled into the hills. If they see a car with an Englishman I'm afraid they might well take a pop. We can't have that. HMG would never forgive me if I allowed a vicar to be assassinated. It wouldn't look good in the papers. That's a shame, I said. I was looking forward to today. Sorry. No dice. But thanks awfully for all you did for poor Moorehouse. Let me give you my card. Perhaps one day I can return the favour. Or if you ever have a spot of bother with any of our chaps, just show it to them. Tell them we are chums. *Major Reginald Thwaite*, it read in gold copperplate. It included his home address in Buckinghamshire and a telephone number. I thanked him and put the card away in my crocodile skin wallet. I made my way back past the ruined houses to the Rolls. The square which had been packed with prisoners was now deserted. The makeshift pen had been cleared away. To my considerable annoyance Abbas was not alone in the car. A figure sat in the rear. I felt this was extraordinarily impudent on my chauffeur's part. I had rented the Rolls for my tour and I looked upon it as my own property. I did not care for Abbas to turn it into a public hostelry. As I approached the door opened and the man inside emerged. I saw that it was the officer with the beard. He walked towards me and shook my hand. I'm very pleased to meet you, he said. I understand from Abbas you are doing a tour of the holy sites. What's more you are a Zionist. That's excellent news. His eyes were deep-set, blue and full of fierce energy. His beard rather set him apart from the other troops. His uniform was a little dishevelled. In fact it struck me there was a queer resemblance to the bandit I had encountered in the house. He looked like an irregular. You know Abbas? That was what most startled me. Indeed, yes. A very good chap. Gives us lots of assistance. And people like you provide the perfect cover. There's nothing suspicious about a chauffeur, eh? Abbas gets about. We'd never win this damned war if it wasn't for intelligence. Look, I'd love to have a chat but things are still a bit hot round here. I have to be off. He strode off and disappeared into a nearby house. I climbed back into the car. Abbas was counting some mils which the officer had evidently given him. I had no idea that he was an informer. It was hard to imagine what information he had that was of value to the authorities. The sites we toured were not exactly strategic – not in the modern age. But then I remembered Abbas would sometimes go off to buy food or visit friends and relatives. Doubtless there was much gossip. Who was that man? I said. Abbas beamed as he put the coins away in a bag, which he then placed in a walnut-panelled compartment under the passenger seat. He locked the compartment and put the key away. That man, sir, was Captain Wingate. A very good man. He started the car up and we glided away. We did not get far. A pair of soldiers waved at us to stop. Abbas was ordered to pull the car over into the shelter of a house. The house where I'd seen the bandit was about to be blown up. Best stay in the car, sir. It will be safer there. You'd be surprised how far débris sometimes flies. We did not have to wait long. A tremendous roar literally made the ground shake. A shock seemed to rush through the metal structure of the car, even permeating my teeth. It delivered a passing thump to my heart. A moment later a boiling dome of white smoke spread across the town. A thousand birds screeched and took flight. Animals of all kinds began barking and braying and mewling. Next I heard the soft pitter-patter of falling matter. None of it was visible. From where we were parked the scene – a sunlit patch of street, some brightly coloured sheets hanging from a window – was unchanged. Poets, it seems to me, ought to have greater acquaintanceship with high explosive. There is great beauty in the massive expansion of dense, ascending smoke.

E

EXCEPT THE LORD build the house their labour is but lost that build it. The Bedouin, poor souls, know nothing of this. At seven thirty that day we set off for Mount Nebo. Abbas was unhappy. He would have preferred to press on to Jerusalem and the sum of money he was owed for his chauffeurship. He had no choice but to obey instructions. My itinerary was always of the free-spirited sort. After a few miles I banged on the glass and made him halt briefly by a stream. The sky was cloudless, the sun incandescent. A large camel train had paused to let the animals drink there and to eat from ancient grain bags. Women were spreading on the stony floor of the stream strips of cloth some fifty feet long. I took two snaps of this picturesque scene. Then on along a road rising up to a plateau where many Bedouin were working the fields. Black tents dotted the area. Entire families were toiling in the heat. A horseman in bright red veil kept watch. The road to Baghdad branched off to my left, tempting me to try the ruins of Babel and Ninevah. But not this year, nor the next, nor the ones after that. A stone cairn and a large whitewashed arrow pointed the way for airmen flying between Damascus and the Euphrates Valley. I could see the railway leading toward Mecca. Aviators, locomotives, donkeys, a motor car – all passing through this spaceless and timeless sphere. Aviators especially, of late. I chuckle as I remember what Bernard told me. About a year earlier Archibald Wavell had called in the Royal Air Force. There was a gang of rebels trapped in the open. The RAF boys had bombed and machine-gunned the blighters.

Somewhere between fifty and sixty oozlebarts were killed. Then it was the army's turn. Mopping up, they called it. Bare and brown grow the lonely hills. But ours was a good dirt road. In a Rolls one rolls along very comfortably. How marvellous it is to get to the heart of nomadic life by such means! I smiled again. A happy day; a happy, happy day. Now, still delightedly smiling, I plunge into the dawn of Christianity. Here lie the remnants of ancient Hesban, the Heshbon of the Old Testament. This, you will recall, was the capital of Sihon, King of the Amorites. A slippery chap! Moses had difficult dealings with him. One cannot help but sympathise. The American School of Oriental Research in Jerusalem believes this section to be the first conquered by the Israelites, after the Exodus from Egypt. Today all that remains are two tumbled columns and a massive sarcophagus. Poignant vestiges of the one true faith. And on a hilltop nearby is a small walled village with a large gateway. This, podgy detestable Abbas tells me (his thick smug face reminds me of the tip of an oiled cricket bat), is the winter home of the nomads. In the summer they drift across these grazing lands. In winter they settle here while their fields are flooded by daily deluges. Bare and brown grow the lonely hills. But ours is a good dirt road and in a Rolls Royce the journey is most comfortable. Suddenly, coming over the crest of a hill, entirely without warning, we found ourselves in the middle of an entire tribe of Bedouin. There were hundreds of people – men, women, adolescents, babies – together with a plenitude of dogs, sheep and camels. It reminded me of a Biblical epic at a picture house. It was like a page ripped from the Old Testament – the days of the Patriarchs come to life. I told Abbas to stop and stepped out to take photographs. A dozen sheiks riding handsome Arab horses traversed this animated mass of humanity. One of them came over and spoke to Abbas. He sounded angry. Abbas informed me that the man did not want me to take any more photographs. I was tempted to ask on what authority but I decided not to. Instead I took out a packet of Camels and offered the sheik one. The man curtly declined it and rode off. Abbas explained that the Bedouin do not have anything like cigarettes. They do not smoke. He suggested we drive on. Not before time. Some of the more forward Bedouin women had approached and were now pressing their faces against the car window. They seemed fascinated by my pale face. I stared back, equally entranced by their perfect white teeth, their tattered black hair, their long, filthy, ragged dresses, which they trail on the ground. One of these women had distinctly negroid features. I threw her a caramel, which only excited the others. I wound down the window on the far side and tossed a handful out. Screeching like crows, the women rushed to seize them. We left them in a cloud of dust. For miles we chugged over a golden desert plateau. This is the Plain of Moab, which Moses knew. It is here that Numbers and Deuteronomy truly come to life. The Jabbok, the Gulf of Arabah, the slopes of Pisgah – you can find them all on a modern map. And Moses gave unto the tribe of the children of Reuben. And their border was from Aroer, that is on the edge of the valley of the Arnon, and all the plain by Medeba. I have always found it a bit rum that Moses parcelled out land that already belonged to others. We came to Madeba. This was Lawrence's HQ for a while. I wanted to see the famous mosaics. They were laid in the sixth century. A church was built over them by a colony of Greek Christians who migrated here in the last century. They came from Kerak, a Crusader stronghold east of the Dead Sea. Abbas went off to find someone to let me inside. He returned with the teenage son of the Greek priest. The youth was quietly spoken and neatly turned out. It was cool and shadowy inside the church. I removed my helmet and sunglasses and left them on a table inside the entrance. With great pride the lad explained the details of the mosaics. I was fascinated by their primitive portrayal of Jerusalem's walls and domes. These were all done out in the flattest lack of perspective. Adjacent are sections of the Holy Land, the palms of Memphis, the Nile. These are not in the right geographical relation. I stooped to take photographs. A horde of small boys appeared all around me. They were silent, inquisitive, barefooted. Having accomplished my mission it was time to go. But the table by the door now bears only my helmet. The sunglasses are gone. Who stole the gentleman's glasses? The priest's son screams in fury. He scrutinises the faces. One is missing. They flee. Oh Christ, to steal in a church! The youth's face is stricken. And from a clergyman, too. I loiter in the outer court and mop my brow. The suspected thief is quickly apprehended. He is dragged towards me. The priest's son has seized one arm, a village woman the other. The boy is screaming as if I am about to execute him. The villagers are screaming too. Put him in jail! Shame on you! Where are the gentleman's sunglasses? The boy sobs that he has never seen the glasses. He insists he is innocent. His scalding tears are too much for me. I plead for his release. It is going to be hard to go through the glaring miles to Jerusalem with unprotected eyes, but no matter. Besides, the thief will never dare to wear his prize. The horn-rimmed Crooks lens would be instantly identifiable. He will never enjoy the soft, muted aspect it gives to the burning landscape.

END OF THE ROAD, said Abbas. The tar macadam fizzles out. Madeba, this barren spot is called. From here to the spur of mountain running out to Nebo and Pisgah the route is a rough track. We must take a Madeba boy with us for a guide, said Abbas. He clicked his fingers and there on our running board stands a sixteen-year-old Arab wearing a long petticoat. His white veil is held by rings of woven black goats hair. His arching nose is a Semitic delight. Impishly, I name him Hobab. Hearing me speak, his eyes gleam with intelligent joy. Yes, I Hobab, he says. He grins, exposing white teeth, five missing. Yes, I said. You are to be our eyes, as Hobab was for Moses in the desert. Yes, boss. He took the seat next to Abbas. The road became stonier and stonier. What jolts! Abbas begins to mutter about damage to his exhaust. We pass another great encampment of Bedouin. My gaze is on higher things. Morning mountain mists, drifting. A land of miragy prospects. A vision of the Jordan Valley. Abbas brakes and Hobab leaps out. The lad wrestles with a huge rock in the middle of the track. I would like to help but my back hurts. Abbas cannot, for it is a matter of his Arab pride. Hobab eventually gets it to budge. We proceed. Three camels stand silhouetted against the sky. This is the same sky that canopied Moses when he stood here looking toward the Promised Land. A promise which he never occupied. This is where we leave sullen Abbas baking in his metal oven. It is time for me to make the ascent. Hobab leads the way. I trudge after him. Nebo stands 2,643 feet above sea level. The silence is deeply spiritual. Suddenly the mood is spoiled. Two Arabs rise up from nowhere, like a noxious emission from a marsh. The taller of these pestiferous twins announces they will guide me to Moses' tomb. I tell them to bugger off (forgive me Lord, for I was hot and irritable that day). They pretend not to understand the vernacular. Fuck off! Piss off! *Scram.* They grin like monkeys. They find me amusing. Nothing I can say, no matter how vile, will deter them. Hobab says nothing. The parasites lope beside us, determined to extract a gratuity. At last we reach a little pile of stones at the summit. I do not require instruction from a malodorous member of a dusky tribe to understand the history of this place. I have read my guide book. I know already that the famous Moabite Stone found not far from here reveals that this place was once a shrine sacred to Jehovah. One of my new friends, mobilising the few paltry scraps of English he possesses, says: Moses, he sleep here. He says it over and over again, as if he was speaking to a mental defective. Moses, he sleep here. Moses, he sleep here. Pisgah, over there. He look to Promised Land. Moses, he no go Jerusalem. He sleep here, Nebo. As if I was a complete idiot, the fellow folds his hands and mimics the attitude of a man in last repose. This deluded wretch is plainly a Mohammedan. He has never once read the Holy Bible. He is laughably ignorant of the facts. For Moses went up from the plains of Moab unto Mount Nebo, to the top of Pisgah, that is over against Jericho; and the LORD shewed him all the land of Gilead, unto Dan; and all Naphtali, and the land of Ephraim and Manasseh, and all the land of Judah, unto the hinder sea; and the South, and the Plain of the valley of Jericho the city of palm trees, unto Zoar. And the LORD said unto him: I have caused thee to see it with thine eyes, but thou shalt not go over thither. So Moses the servant of the LORD died there in the land of Moab, according to the word of the LORD. And he buried him in the valley in the land of Moab over against Beth-peor: but no man knoweth of his sepulchre unto this day. Got that, matey? Moses was buried down in the valley, not up here. And no man knoweth of the whereabouts of Moses' tomb, least of all a pair of bloodsuckers who prey on vulnerable pilgrims. But as well as my word-perfect Deuteronomy I also had knowledge of The Emergency. It was best not to provoke the natives unnecessarily. I therefore managed a tight smile and with heavy sarcasm thanked the fellow for enlightening me in such depth about Biblical lore and geography. I thrust coins at my tormentors, provoking a storm of gratitude. Mercifully, they then scampered back down the mountain path and returned to lie down in their nest of rocks. When they had gone I gave Hobab a hearty clip round the ear. He burst into tears. Since there is nothing more detestable than a sobbing child I gave him a second whack to shut him up. That did the trick. He became mute and all I had to endure was the prospect of his soulful eyes and their tiresome trickling. I turned away. You get an astonishing panoramic view of Palestine from here. Opposite, on the Judaean hills, lies Bethlehem. Five miles to the north are visible the towers on the Mount of Olives. The mystical hills of the Judaean wilderness look like they might melt any moment into sky. Everything seems like mists in a dream country, not points in geography. Farther north rise the mountains Ebal and Gerizim, in Samaria. Galilean Tabor and Gilboa are too hazy to be distinguished. A slight shift of perspective and you are looking down into that most remarkable cleft in the earth's surface, the Jordan Valley. It ends with the deep Salt Sea. This weird body of water looks like a giant blue eye with salt dune lids. A cloud turns it to turquoise; dullness makes it a zircon, and then an opal. From Nebo you see the spur called Pisgah, where is to-day a little church with notable mosaics. A speck in the sky expands into a swooping hawk. A second speck appears, an aeroplane, with the familiar and heart-warming circles of red, white and blue. The drone of its engine deepens. The brat tugs at my sleeve. He seems agitated; points the way down. He seems to be telling me to go. Oh very well. I am hot, tired and have seen everything. I shake him off and begin my descent.

EVERYTHING? NOT QUITE! For a recent bulletin of the American Schools of Oriental Research illuminates the latest discoveries. Within a comparatively small radius of Mount Nebo, a number of Early Iron-Age sites were found, and one early Bronze-Age site. Some date from the thirteenth to the eighth centuries B.C. A few kilometres northeast of Mount Nebo, at Khirbet Qurn Kibsh, an extensive Bronze-Age site was discovered. This could be dated by its pottery to between 2200-1800 B.C. Such data scientifically proves the trustworthiness of the Bible record. All 'a priori' considerations favour acceptance of the Hebrew tradition and its connection with this phase of the Conquest of Moses. The date of Exodus was about 1290 B.C. The Israelites may therefore have conquered Sihon's territory before 1250 B.C. A useful reminder, if ever there was one, that Palestine is a country in which the mystical and the historical constantly strive for possession of one's mind.

S

SILVERSMITHS WERE SEEN by Isaiah, turning out trinkets for travellers when they should have been helping repair Zion's walls. He watched the artists with their fining pots and delicate filigrees of gold and silver. He heard the divine promise. Behold, I will set thy stones in fair colours, and lay thy foundations with sapphires. And I will make thy pinnacles of rubies, and thy gates of carbuncles, and all thy border of pleasant stones. In righteousness shalt thou be established: thou shalt be far from oppression, for thou shalt not fear; and from terror, for it shall not come near thee. No weapon that is formed against thee shall prosper; and every tongue that shall rise against thee in judgement, thou shalt condemn.

SCRAPS OF CONVERSATION can be heard if you linger by the Jaffa Gate. The natives never tire of sitting on the kerb, staring, yawning, chatting, eating round green melons. Swaying dromedaries pass by. Handsome, sturdy young English soldiers stand around in groups, some holding their rifles while others drink bottled beer. An Arab brags about the native soap factory in Haifa. Another Arab predicts the failure of the next Jewish Fair at Tel Aviv. Why are they talking in English? I suppose it is to impress me. I sit on a chair and rest my shoes on a brass-trimmed box, while a smiling boy gives them a good polishing. A nearby member of the Manchester Regiment is telling a new recruit about local traditions. When you finish your duty often nothing has happened. No bombs or anything. So what the driver does then is switch his wheel backwards and forwards to get the wog on the front to roll off. If he's a lucky wog he'll get off with a broken leg. If he's unlucky the next truck coming up behind hits him. But nobody bothers to pick up the bits that's left. We're the masters, right? We're the bosses and whatever we do is right. And anyway once you've shaken a wog off the bonnet you don't want him any more. He's fulfilled his job. It's the same with prisoners. Any you capture you give them a good beating. I met one chap who had a very unusual souvenir. In his cigarette tin he kept this wog's brains! Pretty disgusting if you ask me. It looked like a chopped-up frog. Sometimes you make the wog hold a heavy rock and every time he drops it you beat him. Sometimes, for a laugh, we put bells round their necks and make them dance. Sometimes we tie their balls with cord. Some chaps pull out the wogs' fingernails with pliers. Me, I draw the line at that. Call me squeamish if you must. But everyone has to join in the beatings. And it can be quite good fun. Anything will do. Rifle butts, bayonets, scabbard bayonets, fists, boots, whatever. That's what the oozlebarts get before they go off to the jail. You form two lines of men with pick axes, scabbards with a bayonet inside, rifles, whatever's there, tent mallets, even tent pegs. And you send the wogs through one at a time, through this… What do you call it? Gauntlet. And they get belted and bashed until they reach the other end. Now any that can run when they got to the other end go straight into the police meat wagon and sent down to Acre. Any that die they go into the other meat wagon and are dumped at one of the villages on the outside. I remember there was one poor sod probably your age well I'd heard people say in the past that you could have you eye taken out and cleaned and put back and I always believed it but it's not so because this lad's eye was hanging down on his cheek the whole eye had been knocked out and it was hanging down and there was blood all over his face.

SIN HATH TORMENTED me since my eleventh year. This is a fact I cannot ever escape: an appetite as loathsome as an opium addiction and the foul, shameful labours it sets me to perform. Talk of eyes and eyesight brings it to mind. I have long risked blindness. My cheeks burn with fire, my dog collar tightens around my throat, my hands grow restless. Time for another pill. Two! I am devilish with my risks. Yet shame floods the soiled temple of my body. My descent into beastliness first began in Glasgow. Father took me with him to attend a church convention. It was the first time I had seen a city. The crowds and the racket astonished me. The streets were crowded with honking vans and horse-drawn carts and glistening clumps of dung. The faeces made a deep impression. I was but a lad and not used to urban ways. We stayed in a dormitory attached to a seminary. In bunks. The boy above me, an older teenager, was fat. He farted throughout the long night. The stench descended like a miasma sent by Satan. The seminary had a gymnasium which the boys, a dozen of us, were obliged to attend. Elsewhere on that estate our fathers explored their theological differences. Their soft, pink-cheeked, mutual hatreds were masked with smiles and words of treacle. Or so I imagine. My father was not a happy man. He may have been while mother was alive, I cannot remember that far back. By the time of the Great War, which had been orchestrated by financiers and foreign filth, the planet was awash with Satan's emissaries. *Satan!* There were few pictures. He had horns and a hairy face, like a goat. His favourite posture was to squat. Demons with scales and talons did his bidding. The Bolsheviks belonged to his battalions. Full-breasted sluts with whirling skirts tore wildly at themselves in his presence, exposing their nipples and stretches of plump upper thigh. For understanding, my father said that the Holy Bible and *Paradise Lost* would suffice. To get closer to this intriguing evil one I immersed myself in Mr Milton but gave up a quarter of the way through. I ruefully realised he was not my cup of tea. Mr Wordsworth is altogether more divine, though he largely shuns the theological. Besides, I was young. At that age the works of John Milton were altogether less interesting than those of John Buchan. Had I so expressed myself openly, father would no doubt have frowned. He did not hold with light matters such as novels, which he said were for idlers, shop girls and fools. The Lord Almighty hath given us one book which contains all books, and that should be adequate for any man. Father once caught me reading *The 39 Steps* but assumed it was a Christian primer about the route to personal salvation. His attention was focused elsewhere. His scowl deepened, his brow grew more furrowed. For father the world's sin was bad enough but the innumerable grievous errors of his fellow priests far worse. But this, during those ten days spent in Glasgow, was of little consequence to his son, Donald. We boys were left to our own entertainments, apart from bible classes, services in the chapel and physical training. PT took place every morning at 11 a.m. By this hour it was calculated that we would have digested our porridge. The gymnasium was in a hall beside a playing field. First we changed in a desolate ante-room, putting on navy blue shorts, white vests and plimsolls. After that we trooped into the gym. The first ten minutes were free play, to get us warmed up (it was bitterly cold in that place). Then the instructor, a harsh sour elderly priest we brutally nicknamed Old Nick, made us hang upside down from wooden bars, jump an old horse with split leather flanks, and run on the spot two-hundred times. The dictates of Old Nick were worth it for those sweet minutes of free play. On my first day I clambered up and down the wooden bars along with the other boys. We shrieked like monkeys. It was good fun. But the gym had other entertainments, including half a dozen ropes which hung from the high ceiling. In memory they seemed to stretch almost to heaven. These ropes were thick as a man's wrist and distinctly nautical in character. The huge twined strands of hemp smelled good. They gave an olfactory pleasure akin to that of a newly baked loaf. The first time I brought my face close to one of the ropes I found the experience agreeable. I raised my arms and took hold of the rope. I pulled my body off the ground, holding my legs out straight as if I was going up and down on a swing. The rope pressed against my crotch. I raised one hand and then the other. Slowly I hauled myself higher and higher. The fat boys and the thin boys fell away and I entered a private realm. It made me realise how good it would be to be an angel, floating above people, seeing everything that was going on while no one knew you were there. It was at that moment I realised something astonishing had occurred. My willy had mysteriously turned hard and grown bigger. It was squashed between my stomach, my clothing, and the granite-hard coils of the rope. Such a phenomenon had never happened before and it baffled me. I was eleven years old and in complete ignorance about the development of the male organ of generation. I was unaware it had any other function than for urination. I had carried it through my childhood like a second tongue, floppy and taken for granted. I hung there, agonized with wonder, my very first erection requiring my most urgent attention. The year was 1917. There was trouble in Russia and the Germans had still not been pushed back to Berlin. Father was daily furious about the state of things but his son had more pressing concerns. Sweat formed in my armpits and trickled down my ribs. I could smell its salt tang. And then there was a new development, another outbreak of wonder. I adjusted my position on the rope, hauling myself an inch or so higher. I fervently hoped this might rid me of my uncanny, unwanted tumescence. I dreaded having to descend. When they saw my willy sticking up like this all the other boys would laugh. The PT instructor would have me packed off to hospital. Perhaps my willy was diseased. Perhaps they would need to cut it off to save my life. It was happening to soldiers all the time. You saw them in Glasgow, limbs missing, resting on wooden crutches, holding out caps for coins. That slight change of position helped to put me out of my misery – and create what was, in retrospect, a far greater one. The pressure of the rope just below my glans was enough to trigger what happened next. As I hung there, my body trembled. A tide rose without warning and rushed through me. A shuddering expanded upward and outward from my troublesome little root of flesh. A honeyed surge. Bliss unspeakable. A cascade of delight to make a boy gasp. And then it was gone. Over. Done with. My organ wilted and returned to its old self. I slid down the rope, exhausted and perplexed. Line up boys, shouted the priest. It was time for some exercises on the bars. I couldn't wait for the next day. This time I declined the games of the other boys and headed straight for the ropes. I chose my old friend, the third one along. I hauled myself up and in no time at all I had another erection and another orgasm. I say that now but those words were completely unknown to me at the time. I hung there, straining the last drops of pleasure from my throbbing flesh. My style disturbs me. It has become pornographic. But I know no other way of articulating that which I shall never articulate to a living soul. My book could never be about such matters. No book could be, apart from one published in Paris. No matter. Sin must be frankly acknowledged, even though only in a confessional of one. Let me confess it, Holy Father. Who knows anyway. Who saw it all. Who has infinite mercy for a sinner such as I. For the angel of the Lord tarrieth about them that fear Him and delivereth them. O taste, and see, how gracious is the Lord. Blessed is the man that trusteth in Him. I repeated my ecstasies every day until the conference ended and it was time to return to the Hebrides. On my last session in the gym, my legs bent around the rope, rubbing myself with exquisite delicacy against the rough strands – I had begun to develop a skill – I was aware of the old priest gazing at me thoughtfully. I closed my eyes and shut him out. There was nothing to give the game away. I was just a boy, hanging from a rope. The old priest said nothing. Perhaps he thought he was imagining it. Perhaps I imagined that he thought he was imagining it. Something I have not made clear. There was no mess in my underpants. I did not ejaculate. My physical development was not yet quite ripe enough for the production of semen. These were dry orgasms, barren of matter from any ventricle. They raise, I think, interesting theological questions, though none I think will ever be mooted in a pulpit or at a public gathering of theologians. The sin of Onan involves the waste of seed. Yet I had, as yet, none to spill. Nor were my thoughts filled with lustful desires or images. My pleasures were entirely innocent, wholly free of base matter. Indeed, I tried to discuss them with one of the other boys, Peter from Manchester. I described to him how when I climbed the rope I got a very nice feeling between my legs. I said no more than that, for to have brought my willy into the conversation would have been unseemly. I knew from father that *unseemliness* was one of the world's great vexations. Peter gawped at me through his wire-rimmed spectacles. He said he had no idea what I was talking about. Matters did not – could not – end there. The pleasure which rose in my groin was addictive. In my heart I knew it was wrong. The thought of discussing the matter with father was impossible. I supposed it was a misfortune which afflicted one in a million. Perhaps it was a kind of disease. But reason was no use to me. I had to have more of this luscious explosive feeling. Upon my return home an obvious difficulty presented itself. No rope. It was therefore incumbent upon me to find a substitute. I soon whittled the matter down to three possibilities. In the garden Nora's washing line hung between two stout cast iron poles. They were about the same thickness as a gymnasium rope. The problem lay in utilising these twins of temptation. During the day I was exposed to observation from the house. Initial attempts to climb one of these poles were witnessed either by my father or Nora. They shouted. Don't do that, Donald! You will break it. Break it, forsooth! Me! A mere slip of a lad up against a fine piece of Victorian ironwork shipped and carted all the way from one of smoky Glasgow's nether regions. I abandoned the poles for the time being, without great regret. This was in part because I somehow knew that the wearing of clothes spoiled the sensation. In my bedroom I had found a substitute which was more challenging but which permitted much greater latitude. The wardrobe. It was a massive structure of dark oak, with curved corners. The wardrobe was perfect. All I had to do was go to bed, put out my light, and wait. The inky blackness dissolved into grey outlines, and the wardrobe waited for me with the patience of a lover. Eventually my father came slowly up the uncarpeted stairs. He spent an eternity in the bathroom. I heard the splash of his ablutions, the gurgle of the WC. After that he went into his bedroom next to mine and closed the door. A yellow light leaked out on to the landing. Another twenty minutes and then he said a short prayer. At long last the light went out. I heard his bed creak as he adjusted his posture. Then silence. Soon I would hear him snore. Only then was it safe for me to quit my narrow cot, untie the string on my pyjama trousers and strip naked. My penis was rigid with anticipation long before I had taken three Wagnerian paces to the wardrobe. I reached up on tiptoe and gripped the frame that ran along the top. This frame concealed a shallow trough which was designed for storage purposes. Father kept a suitcase on top of his wardrobe. My wardrobe bore no load, which greatly assisted my monkey-like acrobatics. I hung there, my legs bent, gripping the cold wood. All that touched the curving end of the wardrobe was my own engorged curve of desire. After a matter of seconds the great shuddering sensation came. I continued there, pressed against this dark hard lump of furniture, my arms straining, until the last spasm of pleasure had been forced from my pale body. Then I quietly dropped to the ground, slipped my pyjamas back on, and went back to bed. In 1918 the war ended. That was not the only great event of that year. I should explain that Nora only came to the manse on weekdays. And on Saturdays and Sundays my father was frequently busy with church business. Apart from my necessary presence on the Sabbath, I was left to my own devices most weekends. And what devices! I usually managed sex with the wardrobe three or four times on a Saturday. I had the matter down to a well timed routine. The summer months were the easiest because on very hot days I could get away with wearing a pair of shorts and a singlet. That made it easier to enjoy the wardrobe without fear of discovery. Even on those very rare occasions when someone rang the doorbell while I was mid-spasm, I had ample time to hurl on my two items of clothing and appear moments later, flushed and helpful. I was cunning enough to carry a ball in one hand, as if the visitor had interrupted me during some energetic childish play. How calculating Satan makes us as we seek to conceal our sinning! Yet did not Christ Jesus come into the world to save sinners? And the blood of Jesus Christ cleanseth us from all sin.

ONE SUMMER'S DAY in 1918, something shockingly unexpected happened. Father was five miles down the road at a mothers' meeting in the church hall. The sun blazed down from a cloudless sky, filling the manse with light and little sparkling dust storms. Somewhere in the distance a flock of gulls screeched. A golden hexagon impressed itself against my favourite end of the wardrobe. As I hung there, on the edge of an imminent ecstasy, the warm sun coated my back and behind with glowing honey. Everything that day seems luminous and sharply defined. I pressed my thighs against the warm wood and the volcanic surge began in my loins. And then it happened. To my astonishment, horror and bewilderment, my penis spat gobbet after gobbet of phlegm. The first couple of bolts shot as high as the ceiling, the rest slapped against my face, my chin, my stomach. I hung there until the orgasm was over, then slithered back to earth. I was truly appalled by this savage and beastly turn of events. The evidence of my furtive pleasure was everywhere. My body dripped with it. The wardrobe was slimed with my lust. The high ceiling held two teardrops from the eyes of the all-seeing Almighty. Even as I gazed, a drop fell from the tip of my shrunken penis and landed on the rug at my feet. The wool absorbed my guilt as if it was blood from an innocent I had just stabbed to death. Like any murderer, the first imperative was to clean myself up. I mopped the mess from my body with a handkerchief (a handkerchief which I afterwards burned). I wrapped a second handkerchief around my genitals – I was still oozing a little slime – and pulled on my clothes. A third handkerchief I utilised to rid the wardrobe and rug of the damning evidence. I felt like a spattered killer mopping up after his moment of butchery. The glutinous matter attached to the ceiling was a very different kettle of fish. It was out of reach. I felt that if my father came home now he would enter the room and see at once what had occurred. Those sloppy grey pearls were as thumpingly blatant as Poe's tell-tale heart. In the end I calmed down. The day went quietly on. I got a different kind of grip on myself. I found Nora's longest broom and by standing on a chair I was able to scrape those lewd deposits from the white purity they had sullied with their presence. By the time father came home Donald was a good boy engrossed by an engaging primer on mathematics. Did you have a rewarding day, Donald? Yes, father. But inside, I was acutely anxious. I was worried I was diseased. My genitals were rotting inside from the abnormal usage which I had subjected them to. I could never tell father. He would take it personally. It would break his heart. Satan had wormed his way into the manse itself. Satan had recruited his own son. Nor did I see how I could explain it to any doctor, least of all fierce, bearded Dr McMurdo. The doctor worshipped at our church. He was a friend of father's. And in a long career it was entirely possible he had never encountered such abnormality and wickedness as mine. Even at weddings he never smiled. I wondered if I would have problems urinating. Mercifully, none. I determined to lay off sex and see what happened. The next day my penis was, to all external appearances, perfectly normal. It was another sunny day. I went to church and prayed silently for the Lord to forgive me. I will sing unto the Lord as long as I live, I pledged. I will praise my God while I have my being. I said, I will take heed to my ways: that I offend not in my tongue. I will keep my mouth as it were with a bridle: while the ungodly is in my sight. I held my tongue, and spake nothing: I kept silence. But Old Nick is not so easily caged. After a week I felt as if I would burst, so great was my desire to go back to my old, wicked ways. After ten days I could no longer hold back. I stood, past midnight, naked before my wardrobe. But this time - Satan had whispered a way to avoid detection - I had taken precautions. I put a grey sock over my penis. This time, when I shuddered, the sock caught the catapulted torrent. I mix my metaphors but you will get the picture. That cotton did the trick. Naturally I had to dispose of this sodden article. I hid it in my brown canvas satchel and took it to a faraway place in the hills. There I buried it among the peat. Guilt had returned yet I knew in my heart that I would be forgiven. Yea, in the secret place of his dwelling shall He hide me, and set me upon a rock of stone. Therefore will I offer in His dwelling an oblation with great gladness. The oldest boy at our little school below the mountains was a violent brute named Donald. Although he was a bully he never picked on me. I think this was partly because I had the same name, which in his sluggish, clogged intellect denoted a mystical kinship. Also I was the minister's son, and to strike at me was to strike at a member of the household of the Lord's local representative. To punch Donald McCollum was to risk being bitten by an adder, or for your bicycle to tip you inexplicably into a ditch, or possibly even for your house to burn down. All bullies fear a greater bully, and the other Donald was not a lad to tempt fate. But though this Donald was feared, he was also grudgingly respected. This was because he knew things we younger children didn't. He knew how babies were made, for example. He had also once talked about elections. At least, that's what I thought he said. Donald sniggered and said one day we younger boys would understand. He had elections every night. I was baffled. But I understood, dimly, that this was all something to do with babies. I decide to ask Donald about my very secret problem. I knew I had to approach it in a roundabout kind of way. I couldn't possibly tell him the truth. There was the great risk he would tell the other children and I would be laughed at, and then someone would tell one of the teachers, and then father would get to hear of it. In the end I squeezed a word out of him. *Spunk*. That was what came shooting out of me when I lustfully hugged desirable vertical structures. In later years I diversified. I acted lewdly in the church cock-loft. Around the age of fifteen or sixteen I discovered what butter and fists were made for. And in the Good Book I found a sort of licence for my wickedness. For does it not say in Ecclesiastes (ix. 10.) *Whatsoever thy hand findeth to do, do it with thy might.* This injunction I obeyed, heartily. Several times a day, when the possibility allowed. I strangled like a strangler. My flushed, agonized face might equally have been that of someone being choked to death, or the straining choker. They say that the last pagan emperor died of a wound from a spear that pierced his ribs. But I was wounded by a spear that grew out of my own flesh. I destroyed its edge. I smoothed it and made it soft and small. I rang its neck. I emptied it of life. A day later it was back, pestering me like an ardent doggie, up on its hind legs, prodding me with the hot tip of its tongue.

T

THE CRUSADERS REDEEMED this land. And then General Allenby. From Beersheba to Dan he made his way, then onward through Syria to Cicilia and the Taurus Mountains. The Viscount was a man who knew the bitter cold in the Judean hills. The Viscount was a man who felt the burning heat of arid summer on the plains. Looking back, all his memories were good. Should we be surprised? No. This ancient land fascinates as no other. *All will rejoice at the progress which Palestine has made under the mandate and will wish her Peace and Prosperity.* Allenby wrote that. But the Crusaders came first. And every romantic-minded pilgrim in Palestine owes it to himself to motor south one half-hour from Haifa to Athlit. Here will be found the Pilgrims' Castle of the Crusaders. Here is their final fortress on the coast, which they struggled for nearly two centuries to hold for Christ. And let's face it: every real traveller glows at the prospect of a castle. I have visited many over the years. The rosy ruins of England's Kenilworth, immortalised by Scott. The plump towers of that soulful edifice on the Bosphorus. The cosy little structure that crowns the hilltop picture-town of Roquebrune on the Riviera. I am, I think it can truly be said, a man of the world in this regard. And so, with a sly pinch of the fold of flesh that lies at the base of the abominable Abbas's thick neck – how he squeals! – off we go. Leaving by the south end of Haifa, we run along between the promontory of Mount Carmel and the Sea. More distant explosions and shots. The occasional roadblock. They always wave us through when they spot yours truly. We speed past the German Knights Templar

Colony of Neuhardhof (another tick for my notebook) and by the post-War settlement of Beith Galim. Arabs smile happily at me from their little booths, put there to guard their precious crops. I jot down the evidence of tomatoes, beans and melons. They are unable to buy trees, unlike their Jewish neighbours who have their National Fund to back them. Suddenly, beyond a modern 'Beach Pavilion', the good road fizzles out. Now we have to bump along a dirt track which crosses grazing land owned by the large Arab village of At-ira, at Carmel's foot. Here, huge culverts have been built, to drain the winter floods. Today they are dry and full of boulders. Abbas slows down for an Arab policeman on his sleek sorrel mount. Before him walks a bearded prisoner in rags, hands tied behind his back. The officer intermittently prods him with a thin, pointed stick. Abbas talks to the policeman, who explains that the man escaped from jail. He is a bandit, and will be punished with a beating. I took out my trusty Kodak but the officer objected. We drove on, coming to an unexpected avenue of towering palms. Buildings appeared but it soon became evident they were empty. Lush green vegetation gripped the walls and swarmed in through unshuttered empty windows. Bird droppings soiled the floors of the abandoned rooms. A well had turned into a plume of soaring greenery. Crickets held a loud rally in the weeds. I wondered what calamity had struck this place. I asked Abbas but at first he pretended not to hear, then merely shrugged. I detested him for his shrugs. Loathing increased its volume inside me, like pus. We came to a mountainous region and followed the route along a narrow rock-cut passage. I was still feverish. Vast quarries came into view. They supplied the new Haifa breakwater. Along the railway puffs the morning train from Egypt. It runs through the broad evaporation pans of the Palestine Salt Company.

Some eight thousand tons of salt a year are produced here. But I am not interested in these mundane material matters. I am trailing the footprints of the Crusaders. I seem to hear the clank of spurs against armour-clad legs. I see the flutter of a thousand cross-emblazoned banners. It was his desire to study Crusader architecture that first led Colonel Lawrence to Palestine. The custodian of ruins appears beside my window. He wants to sell me a ticket. It is printed with the reassuring words DEPARTMENT OF ANTIQUITIES. Here the Crusaders selected a promontory jutting into the restless sea, parallel to its greater northern neighbour, Carmel. Massive mediaeval masonry protrudes eighty feet into the burning blue. Here, half-arches take on a natural crenellation, carved by war and weather. Rapier thorns make hard going among the tumbling stones. I am shocked to find that poor Arabs live inside this castle. Their washing dangles by the thirteenth-century walls. The breeze makes them flutter like bright scarlet and yellow pennons. The surf below is lashed into a symphony of siren music. This entire coast is full of charm. Inside the decayed palace I gazed upward. A four-storey structure, the floors long since gone. I was reminded a little of Leicester's Building at Kenilworth. A high, roofless chamber dedicated to vacancy. Here there are columns with heads carved on their bases. Forgotten royalty. Could it be a carven tribute to Berengaria? Some things can never be known. I went on, picking my way over salty rocks. The tide pools held crabs and snail-shells. I went on, past hovels of mud and stone. Tethered dogs barked savagely at the intruding white man. A little girl looked at me and began crying. I was pleased to get to the cactus hedges. This way to the banquet hall. It is cut out of solid rock. On its seaward side are three large openings for doors and windows, with masonry six feet thick, looking directly east across two thousand miles of sparkling Mediterranean. This gorgeous expanse is canopied with pearly clouds. It was from this shore that the knights made their final departure from Palestine in 1291. What pangs, what losses. What gleams from their crosses. Back to the car. Onward along a grass-grown track, between fields of golden *durra* and Arabs cutting wisps. We come to fruit orchards – apples and peach trees. We come to a man guarding his field from an iron bedstead, with burlap thrown over for shelter, and a white sheepskin to step out on. Beyond his melon patch loom wires bringing power from the new station at Haifa. Abbas takes me on into Tantura. There I offer a maple caramel to a little boy. He scowls and shakes his head. He does not know what it is. Later, refreshed, we drive on. Climbing a hilly road we overtake a car loaded with all the worldly goods of an American Jewish family, who have just landed at Haifa. We arrive before them at their destination: Zikhron Ya'aqov, a Jewish settlement founded in 1882. I feel as if I am in a village of Old Testament times. Two-wheeled carts creak off towards town, laden with barrels of ripe grapes for the community winepress. The wine industry brings money from sales abroad to Jews who, not wishing ever to live in the land of their fathers, enjoy drinking its flowing juices. I buy a bottle of white. For the colonists who come here, there is many a western comfort – hard-surfaced roads, a hotel, food shops, soft drinks stands, motor oils, and bus service to Haifa and to Tel Aviv. And on again, for a picnic. Yellow birds fly overhead. A circle of trees on the edge of a field of grain offer a natural pergola for my snack. A suspicious Arab looms nearby. He sees only a tranquil vacationist (I dare not say author!) and returns to watch his field. This is the Plain of Sharon. It looks just as I expected it to look. I finish the wine. Now I am tired, very tired.

Abbas brings me cushions. I take a nap. An hour slips away. Then on, to Binyamina. Here, a savage disappointment. I was counting on going on to Caesarea to see the ruins. Abbas has let me down again. He chose not to mention that this route is impassable. A series of sand dunes make a barrier which motor cars cannot navigate. Abbas has tricked me into taking this road for nothing. I shall make him pay for his folly. I had counted on trailing Paul's footsteps through the city where for two years he lived pending trial. From Caesarea Paul and Luke sailed west to Rome. At Caesarea Philip preached the Gospel. And there Cornelius lived. And Peter put his footprints. And beyond those dunes did Berenice and Agrippa hear the defence of Paul before Festus. Their steps have vanished. And over there the words of the Apostle hang in the ether above the crumbled port of the procurators. Abbas, grumbling about sand, is shockingly ignorant of such matters. I could not help myself: I smacked his scalp, making him yelp with shock. Go see your bloody Arab farmer friends over there. Tell them to get me a conveyance. Muttering, Abbas climbed out. He slammed the door with great ferocity. He returned with the head man, who peered into the car. He took my baksheesh and then revealed he had a wagon and donkey. Excellent! There is no humiliation in a donkey, for did not our Lord ride one? Then, incredibly – the impudence of the Arab is boundless – he says they are not for hire, not today. They are in use. When they are no longer required it will be too late. Six hours over that sand in the afternoon heat is not possible. He suggests we return some other time. Perhaps the Arab police could take me on horseback! This is unbelievable. Abbas chips in. Few travellers come here, he says. And that is that. There is no option but to go back. I feel sick and angry. Here is a wider historical lesson, too.

That so great a capital as Caesarea could so utterly pass from existence, tenanted only by a handful of primitives. Back we go, down the narrow dirt track which is the old caravan route to Egypt. We honk past several trains, made up of fifteen to twenty camels, each laden with either grain or melons. At Tulkarm, a large Arab village, we join the main road to Jerusalem. A strange sight there: a long line of village women guarded by British troops, all half naked, their brown breasts exposed to the sun. Some sort of protest on their part? I ask Abbas, but he does not hear me. We speed on. Many of the homes in this area are made of stone, built with the money received from sale of land to Jews for their orchards. At Ras el'Ein are springs, the headwaters of the Auja River. From here water is pumped to a reservoir, then on up to Jerusalem, in stages, lifted by stations along the way. Later we drive past miles of pipe, which were laid by Arab labour, under English bosses with Jewish contractors. The pumping stations and staff houses and reservoirs are of substantial concrete and guarded by troops. There are roadblocks along the way but when they see a Rolls with a white man inside they drag aside the coiled wire and wave us past. Beside a sign reading JERUSALEM WATER SUPPLY ENGINE HOUSE I spot a devout Moslem kneeling on the ground in prayer. Perhaps he is asking Allah to bless his kinsmen in 'El Kuds' – 'the Holy Town' as Arabs love to call Jerusalem. Or perhaps he still remembers Allenby's December victory here.

TEL AVIV IS a shock. Cream stucco apartments and building blocks. Ice-cream parlours. Shops selling Kodak films and electric sewing machines. Tel Aviv's hundreds of small factories manufacture everything from furniture to teeth. And pills. Lots of pills, sold in little twists of paper.

A beehive of happy industry, supplying all the wares of industry (and medication!) to a population growing so rapidly that even the mayor does not venture to give statistics. Five hundred new Jews a week are said to arrive at Tel Aviv, out of an annual arrival of in Palestine of more than fifty thousands Jews per year, an increase of ten thousand over the previous year. I see sturdy Jewish youths from America and Europe pouring out of buses. They join streams of people flowing into modernistic cinema houses, to see films just arrived from Hollywood. It is a shock to come from villages so primitive that a child does not know a caramel when he sees it, to the luxury of my room in a Kosher beach-hotel. Its floor is covered with oriental rugs. My bed has a satin counterpane, and an electric lamp invites night reading. I succumb to temptation. Spade ran his tongue over his lips and pulled his lips back over his teeth in an ugly grin. His eyes glittered under pulled down brows. His reddening neck bulged over the rim of his collar. His voice was low and hoarse and passionate. I read to the end of the chapter and put the book down. My balcony has a superb view of the Mediterranean and a surf. Late workers enjoy all the fun of a swim. I take comfort from a pale solitary palm tree. It leans towards me, as Mary Appleby once did. Very tall, it towers over the ruins of time. Building stone smothers it from an adjacent yard. This tree whispers of a day, only a few years before, when sand dunes were all there was to Tel Aviv. After dinner, strictly 'kosher', I walked down Allenby Street. Though it is broad, I found it so thronged with happy humanity that it was impossible to gain comfortable footing. Oh yes, we are happy here, a Brooklyn immigrant informs me. Life is hard here, he insists. But we have come to stay. This is the first entirely Jewish city built in nineteen hundred years. My family wants to be part of it. This is our Jewish homeland we have dreamed of for centuries. We have one common ideal – social justice for our brothers. Abbas, needless to say, detests Tel Aviv. As soon as he had deposited me at my hotel he sped off to Joppa (relations of some sort). The contrast between old Joppa and Tel Aviv could not be sharper. And England, if she wants to keep the pages of her mandate as brilliant here as at Haifa, would do well to pour some of the surplus millions of Palestine's budget into repairs along the busy waterfront of Joppa harbour. At least pave the slimy street where ragged porters, arriving colonists, and departing cargoes make a maze of confusion.

I

I ONLY MET Monty once. It happened on the day I went to Gethsemane. I say day, I really mean night. Abbas drove me by way of Herod's Gate. Then on, via the Damascus Gate. The car headlights raked the wall of the new Rockefeller Museum of Archaeology situated at the northeast corner of the city wall. Olive boughs swayed in the breeze in the grove off the Jericho Road. In their midst a handful of tall, stately palms. The night was blue and profound. Sullen Abbas parked by the Garden railings and waited. I set off alone up the steep moonlit path. It ran between high walls enclosing the property of the Russian Church and the Franciscan. The moon transformed the texture of everything. The olive leaves were frosted with silver. Walls became liquid and magical. The path ahead of me was chequered with bright light and deep shadows. No human voice can be heard. No dog barks, or child cries, or donkey brays. Every night He went out and lodged here, in the mount that is called Olivet. Luke said that. A sense came over me that I was seeing what Jesus saw, under this same full moon twenty centuries ago. Over the cleft of the valley rises the city of dreadful night. Jesus came by way of the Dung Gate, of this I am certain. In the full glory of the moon He sauntered along the east wall between the old temple area and the Kidron. The olive trees of Gethsemane supplied shadows for concealment and prayer. Under moonlight such as this it was easy for His betrayers to point Him out. The failure of His closest friends makes one wonder whether anyone is entirely to be trusted. Mussolini is surely right when he says: I suffer so intensely from anything like treacherous conduct that I endeavour to abstain from personal friendships. Devotion to a cause requires abstention from that which others think essential. When I find a friend has been disloyal, says the Italian leader, it is as if I had ashes in my mouth. Life is full of duties to be performed and sorrows to be overcome. Here, the miracle of Christ's character comes to the fore. Behold, thy mother, He said to John from His cross. Feed my lambs, He told Peter on the Galilean shore after His resurrection. From the top I looked back over Gethsemane. The road to Bethany is a ribbon of iridescent silver. Lights show from the Oriental Research building. It holds the newest finds – Late Bronze house-walls and the Astarte porcelain cylinder from 1300 B.C. And then the descent. It was with reluctance that I left this place and went back down the little path leading to the road from Jericho. The descent is never as good as the way up. By the wall of the Franciscan Basilica I could hear men's voices. Later, crossing the Kidron, I noticed a torchlight. It flickered weirdly on a hillside outside the north wall of the city. It brought a shuddering sense of those torches carried on Passover night, when soldiers hunted Christ. The torch moved out into a field, where many were gathered. Some kind of ceremony. Jerusalem is ever a city of mystery. There was a much bigger surprise in store when I got back to the car. Abbas was being held against the Gethsemane wall by soldiers. An armoured car was parked behind the Rolls. As I approached, an officer materialised. He called out my name. I consented to admit my identity. The officer, I recall, introduced himself as Giles. I never got round to asking if that was his Christian name or his surname. He shook my hand. Giles said that I was needed. I scrutinised my wristwatch. The hour is getting late, I said. Your services are needed, he replied, taking my arm. This is most important. It cannot wait. Another dying soldier, I assumed. The Padre must still be in Egypt. Having done one good turn, the army had marked me down as someone to be called upon in an emergency. Oh very well, I said, a trifle peevishly. One cannot refuse to minister to those in desperate need, yet I was feeling tired after my walk and wished for nothing more than a good night's sleep. Giles exposed a mouthful of yellow teeth. You can tell your driver to go home, he added. Very well, I said. Abbas, inscrutable as the proverbial oriental, silently climbed into the Rolls. He drove off. Giles ushered me towards the armoured car. Giles gripped my arm and helped me into it. It was hot, dark and uncomfortable inside. I sat on a metal bench, resting the back of my head against the side. Where are we going? I asked. That I cannot say, said he. For reasons of national security. I quite understand, I said, although I did not. Besides, I did not particularly care where we were going. It was hardly the time to fit in a spot of sight-seeing. The interior of the vehicle was illuminated by nothing more than the pale night itself, seeping in through the observation slits. A street lamp sometimes threw in a quick splash of light. I saw that Giles's jaws were grinding something. Then Jerusalem seemed to depart and now all I could see was the occasional twinkle of a star. I must have dozed off. When I woke some forty-five minutes had passed. I turned to Giles. Where is this man of yours? Is he badly wounded? He said: I really don't have a clue what you mean, old man. I mean the soldier. Didn't you want me to guide one of your men into the next life? Good Lord, no, he said. Then what do you want with me then? It's the Major-General. He wants a word. Now it was my turn to look bewildered. Who? The C in C, he replied. Montgomery. Blood mad, they say the bishop called him. I was nervous but proud to be summoned. Why? You'll soon find out. We're there. The armoured car halted and Giles helped me out. We were in a vast military base. All around were low wooden huts and long rows of army lorries. The perimeter fence was lit by spotlights. It was somewhere in the desert. I had no idea where I was. Giles led me towards a nearby wooden bungalow. A flag drooped from a pole attached to a chimney. There was a lot of smoke rising up from the distant hills. Two guards saluted as we approached. Giles led me up some steps and inside. In the hall there was a table with a soldier sitting behind it, reading some papers. He said to Giles, He's waiting. Giles nodded. Just go on through that door. The Major-General is expecting you. I did as commanded. A short corridor led to another door. I opened it and went in. A figure sat in an armchair, holding a cut glass tumbler and staring out through the window at the view. It consisted of floodlit tennis courts, a football pitch and a distant wire fence. Monty heard me come in and sprang up. Dr McCollum? Please, join me. It was good of you to come. A glass of whisky? I don't normally touch the stuff, he quickly explained. But tonight I am letting my hair down. Or I would if I had any! He barked at his own wit. He was merry that night. I said I would, yes. It's a damned fine malt. He looked at the label. An Islay malt. The best there is. He glared at me as if I had disagreed with him. As a Scot I cannot disagree, I said. We clinked glasses. I expect you're wondering why I asked you here, eh? I admitted that I was somewhat puzzled. I described the earlier episode involving the dying soldier and explained about the misunderstanding. Monty laughed. Not dead yet, he said gruffly. His accent was marinated in English privilege. A golden syrup had lubricated his ascent to what he was. He was absolutely certain of his absolute certainties. I had and have no objection to this. It is what faith requires of any man. And yet. Monty seemed to manifest from another world, and in a strange dialect. What let him down was his face. The nose reminded me of a rat. The eyes, too. They held a certain dark calculation. Lately, on the newsreels, he has taken to wearing a beret, like a Parisian harlot. I must say it rather suits him. His head was bare that long night we shared together. At one point, towards midnight, to my amazement, Monty embraced me. We had been reminiscing about this and that, and speaking of how time marches on. Monty spoke in segments. He chopped his sentences into little nuggets of fact and belief. It is my belief, he said, that we are in for a war with Germany. I found this hard to believe. Germany and Great Britain seemed to have so much in common. However, I did not like to disagree, so I nodded as if in assent. Monty and I talked some more. The clock ticked past midnight. Time – nothing – disturbed him. I was enthralled to be with a great man. I can truly say that I was only aware of a fraction of what passed that night. The reason for our conversation emerged gradually. He was lonely. He needed to speak freely to a man of the cloth. A man who would hold his tongue. I was his confessor. Past midnight, and two tumblers later, he put his arms around me. He began sobbing. I was amazed and perturbed. His tears trickled down, to be absorbed by his wiry moustache. I could see glints of ginger in among the black, freshly trimmed hairs. Bernard is a good name for a man with a moustache. It has something of hairiness about it. Monty's tears did not cease. I miss her so bloody, bloody much. He was speaking of his deceased wife. I have forgotten her name. Brenda? Betsy? Something along those rugged lines. B and B in a B & B? Improbable, ridiculous, my mind's wandering. Monty gripped my knee, then let go. To find death in Burnham on Sea, he said. Of all bloody places. Vinegar, fish and chips – they smell of it. Death. They are ruined for me.

They will always stink of her dying. Fish make me sick. I'm a meat man now. Beef, chicken, bangers. His face was wet with his continuing grief. And the gulls, he said. Howling like fallen angels. Have you ever looked at the eyes of gulls? They remind me of the Japanese. They have cruelty embedded in them. They are not human. One day we shall have to smash the Japs too. You mark my words. Monty smiled at the thought. It was a good, pleasing thought. Another whisky? Don't mind if I do. Then, abruptly, he pulled himself together and retreated into his carapace. Keep all this to yourself, he said. It isn't the sort of thing I'd want to get out. It would be very bad for morale if the men got to hear of it. Nobody wants their commanding officer to be a milksop. I shall never tell a soul of this, I said. As God is my witness. He was all dried up inside, I felt. Bereavement had withered him. I have seen it happen several times. The dead sucking all the life out of the living. Monty checked his buttons. He need not have worried. They were all done up. But no matter how correct his uniform, it could not mask the mortal man beneath. Monty smelled of sweat, plus a strange musty smell, as of moths. A strange tang of odours. Perhaps he did not wash often enough. A general's life is a busy one. Ablutions must seem like a gross and futile indulgence. Myself, I try to bathe at least twice a day if at all possible which it isn't always when you are in one of the barbarous regions of the world. To be honest I am a bit of a stickler for hygiene and order. The old saying that cleanliness is next to godliness is too easily sneered at. Monty's head tipped forwards and he stared silently at the rug. The pattern involved peacocks and oranges. The Palestinian sun had faded it. The oranges were barely orange at all. They might have been tennis balls. He did not react as I got to my feet. I need to take a leak, I said. Monty said nothing. He was still engrossed in his rug. I followed my nose and found what I was seeking. The Major-General's lavatory was deliciously enticing to a man who had not defecated for over eight weeks. It was Spartan but spotless. A faint tang of Flit perfumed the spacious room. The bolt on the door was a sturdy one. That calmed my natural anxieties. On one wall hung a framed photograph. I recognised Monty. He looked a lot younger. He was standing beside an antique cannon, looking very serious. On the far side of the thick black barrel stood a fellow officer. Both were clutching canes. In the background was a large, pale building resembling an apartment block of the sort Dostoevsky lived in. I guessed it was a passing out photograph. I dropped my trousers and underpants and lowered myself on to the wooden seat. If I was ever going to loosen my bowels in the Holy Land this was surely the place. But it was no go. I even doubled-up, so that my nose was almost touching the linoleum floor. I pressured my muscles and felt my sphincter open. The lino had a brown marble pattern. I strained and strained and felt my sphincter writhe. Its puckered lips opened wide, then closed again. It was like opening a door and encountering a brick wall. Not even the sight of a neat pyramidal heap of cannon balls in Monty's picture could inspire me to lay down my own dark deposits. I emptied my bladder and accepted defeat in the other quarter. When I returned, Monty became formal and correct. He did not advert to his earlier emotional outburst. It was as if he wanted to crush it with fresh facts. Let me tell you about what we're up to here. But you mustn't put it in your book. Mum's the word, eh? His revelation startled me. You know about my book? Monty's eyes held a merry twinkle. Oh, we know all about you, Dr McCollum. I wouldn't be talking to you like this if we didn't. Intelligence, you know. No army can do without it. As we were moving onto military matters I told him about the prisoners I'd seen in Acre. He gave me the true figure. His tongue explored his moustache. His eyes glowed. Don't believe what you read in the newspapers. What's happening in Palestine is not a national movement. These people we are up against are bullies. We are smashing them. That's what The Emergency is all about. Thank God for Munich. Chamberlain is not the fool people think he is. Munich gave us a breathing space to get the job done here. Munich freed up eight divisions. We could never go to war in Europe with unfinished business out here in the Middle East. But the job is nearly done. The Arabs have been smashed. It's just mopping up, now. Soon I'll be on my way back to blighty. To be honest, I shall be glad to see the last of this damned place. I'm more of a tanks man. I have always been interested in tanks. I remember the first girl I ever fell in love with. I went walking with her on the beach. I showed her how to win a tank battle. I marked it all out in the sand. And you know what? She wasn't interested. I begged her to marry me but she turned me down. It is all very sad. She was too young to appreciate me. She was a teenager and I was in my thirties. It was nearly all up for me when I met Betty. Married at thirty-nine! A close shave, that was. But we rubbed along pretty well together. And then she died. Bitten by an insect on the beach. So you see, father, beaches have never brought me luck. Nor me, I said. I once slipped on some seaweed and sprained my ankle very badly. In Fife this was. But Monty wasn't listening. He had gone deep inside himself. There, all he could find was a Major-General. Monty – this is pretty generally known nowadays - could not pronounce the letter 'r'. He talked of how the Eighth Division would blake the Awab wesistance. I have gwate confidence in the outcome, he said. At times his voice was so squeaky I yearned to oil it. But that night the lubricant was hot foamy saliva and malt whisky and ice which cracked like little pistol shots as it melted in our cut glass tumblers. Monty was not embarrassed by his oddities. He had the tranquil confidence of a Bishop's son. I suspect he never masturbated after fourteen. He had an iron grip on his proclivities. Discipline is required in the army as well as breeding. His scrotum must have been bloated like a double-balloon with all that unspilled desire. No doubt he dreamed, as do we all. No doubt that girl on the sand dragged him down and undid her buttons and let him lick and fondle her schoolgirl's breasts. No doubt he woke in the darkness to find himself spouting like a whale, his body folded over. But no man of restraint can avoid a sticky situation like that. God sees all but is indulgent towards *frottage* induced by dreams. Grey flakes of guilt cling to the stripes of many men's pyjamas. Monty's batman is, I am certain, very discreet. You do not, must not, ever, mention the soilings of a hero. If my book was to mention Monty at all – it will not – he would cross its puny stage with the solemn tread of a Caesar. I would not presume to do anything other than worship the Prince of Peace and the men who must ensure, with tanks if necessary, His continuing rule over the dark and barbarous lands of the world. I am not a sneak. I breach no-one's confidences. You will not find me scattering little barbs of innuendo amid a well laid-out arrangement of subordinate clauses. Then, with a lurch of his body, the Major-General was back with his wildness and grief. Let me tell you something else, doctor, he said. Monty leaned closer and put his hand on my knee. His breath was stale. I ate a melon once, he said. I swallowed a mouthful of seeds. Now I have a tree growing inside me. A tree in my stomach! I feel its branches, rustling against the lining inside me. It is horrible.

I do my best to forget it. I think about tank turrets, for example. Their design could be improved. And another thing. I had a strange dream last night. I was living in a rented room. I went to draw the curtains over the living room window when a mouse scampered along the top of the curtain. It reached the end and dropped to the ground. The mouse appeared in a weak and distressed state. I seized a large hardback book and slammed it down on the mouse, crushing it to death. The doorbell rang. A crowd of visitors entered. Some of them sat on the sofa. At the feet of one of them lay the book, with the dead mouse beneath it. Everyone chattered gaily and no one seemed to notice the dead rodent. And then I woke up. That is indeed a strange dream, I said. I stood up, in order to liberate my knee. I did not wish to be unduly suspicious. I did not wish to give offence. But neither did I wish to be regarded as one who might, perhaps, have homosexual proclivities. If Monty was performing a test, I was determined to fail it. I did not hold it against him, if that was his way. Soldiers spent months together, cooped up, sweating, limb against limb. In the dark one hole is much the same as another. This is a vice common in some quarters of the priesthood. Communion wine, lads with glorious voices and flawless skin and rosy cheeks… I can understand how some might slither into buggery. My vice is altogether more solitary. I do not require another personage to taste bliss. Coupling holds no appeal. I stood by the open window and put my head out. The tennis court lights had been switched off. Now there was merely the distant incandescence of the lit perimeter fence. The stars were, as always, far brighter than at home. They shimmered and blazed like liquid silver. I lack the words to do better. And then I heard it. A sudden ululation. A strange cry of grief. A woman's tongue. It began as a low howl, as I have heard from wounded dogs. It quickened into a fast, raw sob of grief and despair. It must have come from a nearby village, via some strange acoustical effect. It thickened and grew louder until it seemed to fill the whole of Palestine. And then it was drowned out by a surge of music. Behind me, Monty had put a 78 on the gramophone. A lively orchestral piece which I did not recognise. Elgar, he said. The *Cockaigne* overture. A tiny froth had formed at each corner of his mouth. It reminded me of the yellow clots of air and water that cling to the strand's edge on a blustery day at home. I do not particularly like Elgar, although I can quite see why a military man might. *The Manual of Military Law*, 1929, is a real boon, he said. The regulations state quite clearly that inflicting suffering upon innocent persons is indispensable as a last resource. The existence of an armed insurrection justifies the use of force necessary effectually to meet and cope with the insurrection. Beaming, Monty began to conduct the orchestra. The Eighth Division has thirty-five garrisons and detachments, he said. But don't put that in. I won't, I said. On that you have my most solemn word. Monty nodded. I am charged with maintaining order in the area of Samaria, Galilee, and the whole of the frontier district. What we are up against here has been nothing less than a campaign run by professional bandits. They take their orders from Damascus. You know what we did? We got Charlie Tegart over from India. A no-nonsense chap. He set up Arab Investigation Centres. When a wog goes into one of those places he gets the third degree. It doesn't take him long to spill the beans. It is the only way with these people. As for the wog ringleaders… We deport them to the Seychelles. Get the bastards out of the way. Monty chuckled. He liked a good joke. His voice was again so squeaky I yearned to tip syrup down his throat. His face composed a smile. His eyes twinkled. You might say we left them to develop their Seychellist ideas out of harm's way. I grinned, appreciating his wit, though I rather thought he had told the joke before. Another joke: There was this Awab chap who put in a complaint that one of our lads had beaten him. He was able to identify the man. He said it was soldier number 65. The tears streamed down Monty's cheeks as he reached the punchline. The fellow didn't wealise that evewyone in the York and Lancaster Wegiment has the number 65 on their helmet! I smiled politely while Monty dabbed his cheeks with a spotless white hanky. That's because it used to be the 65th Foot, he added. This Awab didn't understand that none of our men cawwy any identifying numbers. They are not policemen, for heaven's sake. His face went back to fierce. Their esprit-de-corps is a gang one, he barked. I think he meant the rebels. These gangs consists of anything from fifty to one-hundred and fifty men. But with God's support, and that of the RAF, we have smashed them. And we do not neglect the small things that can really count. We ban all journalists from operational areas. Journalists lack the true patriotic spirit. And we pay four pounds for a captured rifle. A tidy sum to a peasant and well worth turning informer for. And we hang anyone found in possession of ammo. A single round merits execution. That puts the fear of God into them, I can tell you. Our lads know what their duty is. Bash anybody on the head who breaks the law. If a chap won't be bashed, he must be shot. It's a nice, simple objective and the soldiers understand it. It's also popular. All ranks enjoy a bit of argy-bargy. Monty fell silent. His face took on an introspective expression. He was tumbling back into the dried-up wells of his past. Goodness, is that the time? I must be on my way. Monty did not attempt to detain me. A cock was crowing out there in the darkness. The tennis courts were pale rectangles. I have told no one of this night. It would sound outlandish, even imaginary. Even in my own mind it bears the lurid edging of a dream. That a man like Montgomery should pour out his heart to a poor sinner such as me. Stranger things have happened in history. Or should that be History? In the ante-room the same grey man was still scrutinising the same grey papers. I saw the names al-Bassa and Halhul. He had a large block of India Rubber, a pot of ink and several sheets of stained blotting paper. Giles was slumped on a wooden chair, his head tilted forwards. The grey man produced a walking stick from below the table and used the ferrule to prod Giles awake. He started, saw me, muttered something, and was gripped by a series of yawns. Giles rubbed the sleep from his eyes and escorted me to a military water tanker parked outside the bungalow. This chap will take you back to Jerusalem. I've told him where your hotel is. He indicated a corporal with blazing blue eyes and a set of unusually white teeth. Thanks awfully for coming. I'm sure the C in C appreciated it. Well, cheerio! Giles gave a friendly wave and went on waving until the dust rising from our wheels erased him.

N

NOT THAT MONTY was the only great man I encountered in Palestine. There was one other. It would be invidious to compare them – a pineapple is no better than a pomegranate, after all – but it would be fair to say that if Monty was simply a man who had a job to do and got on and did it, the other man was possessed of more than a sense of duty – he had a mission. But of course I cannot – shall not – mention them in my book. The publisher was quite clear that there must be no mention of The Emergency. The book was to be an uplifting tale of travel to a region both divine and colourful. The natives should appear at regular intervals but strictly in roles which were comical, poignant, amusing and delightful. The reader would not expect negativity. The reader would not want unpleasantness. The reader requires edification and entertainment. A shepherd walks at the head of his flock, with an injured lamb draped around his shoulders. Describe his curious adornments. As he walks he talks to his obedient flock, in a loud sing-song voice. He is using a weird language unheard of in Tonbridge Wells. The words were animal sounds arranged in a kind of order. But that is not all. Early one morning I saw an extraordinary sight not far from Bethlehem. But I shall save that for the book. It was in Haifa that it occurred, this episode which I shall not mention. My zig-zagging around Palestine was just about complete. By now I had all the material I needed. I had only returned to Haifa to take some photographs. I was sauntering along one afternoon when a big dark car cruised alongside me like a shark. For a dreadful moment I thought I was about to be assassinated. The man at the wheel was glaring at me and I could see a revolver on the ledge below the windscreen. The car braked sharply and the man called out my name. It is Dr McCollum, is it not? It is, I replied, half-dead from terror. And then I realised from the fellow's beard that this was the chap I had previously encountered in Sabastia. Hop in, he said. I thought he was offering me a lift and I was touched by his kindness. Far from it. We're one man short, he said somewhat later. First he drove me out of town. Where are we going? To a settlement. Don't fret. The name doesn't matter. It's what we're going to do that matters. For righteousness exalteth a nation. Wingate pointed at the fields. This is their *Altneuland*, their old-new land. The Jews are loyal to the empire, he said. You would be amazed to see how they have made the desert blossom like a rose. Intensive horticulture everywhere. Such energy, such faith, such ability, such inventiveness as the world has not seen. Palestine is essential to our Empire. Our Empire is essential to England. England is essential to world peace. That is why we must ruthlessly suppress any attempt at opposition. Islam is out of it, out of it, out of it.

NIGHT IS SWEETER than day, old warriors say. So too for the moulding of Zion. Captain Orde Wingate saw to that. An odd name, Orde. Short for Order? Hayedid - The Friend. That is what the Jews called him. His detractors – there were many – had other names. One sneering fellow even whispered it was short for ordure. I must confess that the malice in men's heart sometimes astounds me. For that was what the Captain imposed, order. I admired him for that. There is too much chaos in the world. It is the duty of civilised Christians to root out malevolent and mercenary manifestations and set it to rights. Captain

Wingate said: Are you interested in cars? I said I was not. Pity. This is 1937 Studebaker convertible. A real beauty. The yanks make far better autos than the English. He accelerated, blowing the horn at a shepherd with his flock. The bleating sheep scattered and ran off across the dusty plain. I looked back. The shepherd was shaking his fist and screaming. A hoot! We sped along the dusty, empty road. Wingate drove much faster than hideous Abbas. He held on to the wheel with one hand and made gestures of a swooping plane with the other. This was in connection with an anecdote about a radio truck. Whenever they had a spot of bother they called in the RAF. The Hawker Hart biplanes dropped their bombs. Result: fourteen dead oozlebarts. Wingate laughed and accelerated. Twenty minutes later we turned off onto a dirt track that led across a hillside dotted with pine trees. In the distance a stockade and a watchtower. This place seems alive. It is very lovely at this time of year. The settlement had taken over an Arab house, which the owner in Bagdad had sold to the JNF. The tenants had been given the order of the boot. It housed ninety kibbutzniks. They had submachine guns and an Austrian-made Schwarzlose heavy machine gun. Technically the Jews are not allowed such weaponry but the authorities turn a blind eye. Whereas if an Arab is caught with a rifle we hang him! Wingy laughed and I laughed too. I was startled to find British troops living alongside the settlers. They were housed in a pair of wooden huts, twelve men in each hut. Theoretically. But one hut held only eleven. One of the soldiers had contracted an ailment of the groin and was absent. His chums were lounging around playing cards and smoking as we arrived. Wingy led me into his quarters, a small bungalow. He poured us both a whisky. And then another. He asked me a number of questions about my faith, the

Bible and my commitment to a Jewish state. I answered them to his satisfaction. With that out of the way he started to tell me about the SNS. The Special Night Squads were his own invention. They took the war to the enemy. You marched by night and caught them on the hop. In person they are feeble, he said. Like all ignorant and primitive people they panic easily, he said. Outcome: lashings of dead oozlebarts. And you know what? It was all my idea. But those bastard Arabists back in London hate me for it. They have conspired against me. They have taken away my command. You mark my words. In the end they will shut down the SNS, the cunts. These are the first soldiers of the Jewish army, he said proudly. That's what those bastard Arabists hate. But it's too late now. They have the training and the weaponry. Soon the time will come for them to seize Palestine. I shall be there. In the meantime I must wait. Tonight is my last patrol. My last crack at those fucking Arabs. He grabbed hold of my wrist. Come, let us sing. Kneel. We kneeled. One here will constant be, we sang. Come wind, come weather. A glorious melody. And now we must get you sorted out. *Equipped.* Equipped? Didn't I say? We're one man short. This is the chance of a lifetime. Help build Zion. But I can't shoot a gun, I said. I know nothing about weapons at all. Don't worry, he said. Sergeant Russell will help you out. Wingy had a field telephone on his desk. He picked up the receiver and cranked the handle. Sergeant Russell appeared. He was a big fellow. This way, sir, he said. He led me to a hut where he showed me a bolt-action Lee-Enfield rifle. I don't think I'd be much good with that, I said. Perhaps you're right, sir. How about this? He handed me a revolver. That looks just the ticket, I said. He loaded it for me and showed me the safety catch. That's all you need to remember, sir. Don't worry about reloading. One of the chaps will do that for you if we ever get that far. Which we may not. Some nights we go out and come back without killing a soul. But we hope to do a bit better than that tonight. Make it worthwhile for the C.O. As it's his last patrol. A crying shame if you ask me. Sergeant Russell gave me a canvas pack and a helmet which felt too tight. I went back to the bungalow. Wingy was whistling in the kitchen. He was starkers. I naturally assumed he had stepped from his ablutions. Not so. Nudism was his domestic orthodoxy. Orde has very deep set eyes, periwinkle blue. Aquiline features. A faraway, wild look. A bit scruffy. The face of an ascetic. A man with a vision. A very tiny cock. He is clearly one of the instruments of God's hand. Get some rest, he said. I did. I was glad to be away from his naked presence, it perturbed me. For a terrible moment I thought the entire British army was officered by rampant homosexualists. This was an uncharitable suspicion. The naked truth emerged later. Night fell. I slept. I woke with a terrible thirst. I lay there for some time, half asleep. I was parched but paralysed. The effort required to get out of bed and look for a tap was too enormous. But in the end I could lie there no longer. I rolled out of bed. I stood and padded to the door with the slow movements of a somnambulist. Not that I have ever seen a somnambulist (but I have read about them in crime novels). My bedroom opened onto the lounge. I passed through it into the corridor at the far end. A light gleamed under a door. I gently raised the latch and gingerly opened it. It was not the kitchen, nor was it a bedroom. It was some kind of store room. Packing cases were heaped against the wall. A single bare bulb hung from the ceiling. A moth fluttered around it, lunging at the bulb. On the far wall, which was bare, hung a large reproduction of the Virgin Mary. I assume it was the copy of an Italian renaissance painting. It wasn't one I recognised but the

Virgin's face was in the Mona Lisa tradition. She had a pert smile and impudent green eyes. Her face was cushioned by a small, sensual double chin. The yellow glow around her scalp seemed at odds with her slut's demeanour. Wingate was crouched naked on all fours before Her. No, not on all fours. His left arm supported him as he kneeled like a cat, but his right hand was attending to his groin. The rhythmic movement of his elbow left me in no doubt as to the nature of his worship. He moved his hand towards his face and opened it, spitting into his palm. The lubricant was then transferred to the appropriate location. His thin, rather bony backside shivered a little, as if rocked by a passing breeze. Wingy whispered something hoarse and passionate and inaudible, then sighed three or four times. He dripped like a candle. The time for self-restraint is past, he said. But that was later, some hours after I had gently closed the door to the store room. I do not think he was aware of my presence, although in later years I have wondered if he was and if the performance was staged for my benefit. Later I was roused from my fresh slumber by Sergeant Russell. Time to go, sir, he said. I'll be ready in a jiffy I said. The bed sheet had fallen to the floor. I blushed. I fervently hoped that the Sergeant had not noticed the tumour lying across my stomach. Where did we go that night? It must have been across the triangle of death, of that I am almost certain. But geography has never been my strong point and in this place one name can easily get tangled with another. I remember vividly the tremendous raucous unending din of frogs. I remember moonlight shining on a placid silent lake, turning it to a sheet of mysterious silver. The stars were close enough to pluck from the sky, like heavenly fruit. Our mission was preceded by a pep talk. I felt it was addressed as much to me as to the others. The military strength of the whole

Arab group is quite negligible, he said. The potential military strength of the Jews is equivalent to at least two British army corps. Islam in reality cares little about the Arabs of Palestine. In any case, Islam today has no strength. Strength is what counts. Force. Might. He spoke quietly, with complete conviction. We must ruthlessly suppress the Arabs. We must recognise the right of the Jews to emigrate to Palestine. We must advance the foundation of an autonomous Jewish community. For the Jews are loyal to the Empire. And we are instruments in God's hand. Together with the Manchesters, the Royal Ulster Rifles and the Royal West Kents. Wingy became reflective. I felt like a disciple, sitting at the feet of The Master. He stared into the darkness. He focused his gaze on yours truly. After Chaim was killed by a mine, he said, we went to the Arab part of Beit Shean. We beat everyone we met. We went into the shops and smashed them up. Some of the young men resisted. We shot them like dogs. Getting shot is nothing. I myself have been shot five times. There was no damage to speak of. I must have pure blood. Tonight, he said, we go out for the last time to protect the Iraq Petroleum Company's pipeline between Kirkuk and Haifa. The rebels are shooting holes in it every night and setting light to the leaking oil. We shall kill every Arab we find near the pipe. This is holy work. God gave it to us to slay the enemies of the Jews. For the enemies of the Jews are the enemies of all mankind. There was a mutter of approval from the assembly. We readied our weaponry. The bayonets were sheathed in cloth. Corks were placed on the tips. Wingate wore twin revolvers, hanging from a belt, cowboy style. I can make little sense of what happened that night. We walked for three hours without talking. Finally we came to a village. We surrounded it and opened fire. Screams, shouting, confusion. I fired a single shot. The recoil hurt my wrist. I suffered for twenty-four hours. We took prisoners, some youths. Wingy forced sand into the mouths of some of them. One, who was insolent, he shot dead. We set fire to half a dozen homes and then set off back to our distant stockade. The others went off to sleep. I remained in the bungalow with Wingy. He had stripped off, now. I tried to avoid looking at his genitals. A faint smell of excreta hung in the air. He poured us both whiskies. He drank the first one down in seconds and poured another. They say they don't need us now, not after Munich. He sounded bitter. Did you know that the deal with Hitler released eighteen infantry battalions? I did but I did not say so. They are smashing the Arabs and then they will carve up Palestine. They plan to give only a fraction to God's chosen people. Soon will come the time to declare war on the English! His face was pale, his eyes burned. He clenched his fists. We shall blow up the Haifa oil refinery, he whispered. The time for self-restraint is past, he said.

E

ENDINGS ARRIVE UNEXPECTEDLY, sometimes. Bolts of lightning, ships hitting rocks, reckless drivers. To name but three of the fatal sort. Others involve attendance by clumsy polka dot costumed clowns wearing gigantic footwear. Lately my hands have begun to shake uncontrollably. The pills muffle the thunder in my head but do not rid it of the storms. I sweat and burn like a soul in purgatory. I have difficulty holding a pen. I cannot sleep. My thoughts turn to extinction. Flesh lets us down in the end, with its decrepitude and infections and noxious emissions of fluids, slush and gas. All self-control is lost. Your teeth drop away with the years. Drool forks your curling chin. By that final year I hope I will have learned some wisdom. *For man walketh in a vain shadow, and disquieteth himself in vain: he heapeth up riches, and cannot tell who shall gather them.*

NEAR THE END of my time in the Holy Land, in Jerusalem of all places, there was a rather disagreeable scene. Abbas knew I was shortly to depart and broached the question of payment. I solemnly assured him he need have no anxieties on that score. A Scotsman is true to his word. I might have added: So, too, is a soldier of Christ. As my last day grew closer Abbas began – there is no other word for it – to pester me. He was anxious that I should visit my bank and withdraw the necessary sum. I must confess I began to resent this importuning. It had a wheedling quality. His voice began to pipe and squeal. To be perfectly frank, I was beginning to detest the fellow.

The end came suddenly. I had only one day left. Abbas began to blab that he must go back to his wife. He needed his money. *Please, boss.* He was practically weeping. It was as if he did not trust me, which I found extraordinary after all we had shared together. He tugged at his beard, which I may not have mentioned before. It had a luxuriant quality. He reminded me of a somewhat sooty Father Christmas. We were by the Mandelbaum Gate, so-called. Exasperated beyond measure by the latest whining demand for payment I opened the car door and got out. Abbas seemed startled. I said very calmly, Goodbye, Abbas. I could have sworn his dusky skin went pale at these words. He sprang out. He extended his hand, his palm open. You pay me now, Mr Umcullum, sir. I contemplated reminding him that the accurate mode of address would have been *doctor*, but somehow this seemed by the by. I would overlook the assault on correct pronunciation. There are some things one cannot expect of an aborigine. Besides, the chief thing was to be shot of this vexatious litigant. All around us life went on. A camel passed. A donkey trotted past, depositing some cakes of gleaming dung on the dusty carriageway. Women in black with veiled faces glided by. I reached into my wallet and gave Abbas the sum agreed in Cairo. He scowled at the bank notes and hurriedly thumbed through them. I must say I found this a little surprising. It was as if the fellow did not trust me. Can you believe what happened next? The fellow had the insolence to say that the amount I had given him was less than half that which he had been promised! It was a preposterous and absurd suggestion. I am sorry to say that Abbas had patently reverted to what he had always been, and which my natural human sympathies had foolishly obscured from me – a sly, cheating native. Can you believe he not only demanded more than twice what I had so generously handed to him, he also had the amazing impudence to say that a gratuity might also be in order. In short, he wanted no less than *three times* the sum I had given him! It was unbelievable. I was truly shocked that a man I had come to think of as a friend was now displaying that ugliest of all human emotions – naked greed. He even claimed that the money I had given him barely covered the cost of the petrol. This was another manifest absurdity (not that I have ever been someone particularly interested in matters connected to petroleum!). Now look here, I said in a very firm voice. You'll get what you are given and be damned grateful for it. Abbas's response was quite astonishing. He began to shriek. He let loose a torrent of incomprehensible Arabic, which I immediately understood to be savagely uncomplimentary. To my alarm, people were beginning to stare. The street vendors were staring. The shopkeepers were staring. Even a pair of passing nuns had stopped and were staring. (I have never particularly liked nuns. And these, like all the ones I have ever encountered, were spectacularly ugly.) Abbas raised his fist. For a hideous moment I believed that he was about to assault me. A crowd had gathered, evidently fascinated by the sight of an Arab adopting a physically threatening posture towards a white man. I felt a looseness in my bowels. I could not believe that a man of God such as myself could suddenly find himself at the mercy of a violent brute. Luckily help was at hand. God bless the British army! A pair of fine strapping English privates had wandered over from wherever it was they had been. Is this wog causing you trouble, sir? Ah, the rich, homely, delightful accent of Birmingham! I nodded. I said I was sorry to have to say that he was. In fractured English Abbas began screaming that I owed him money. The soldiers looked at each other and laughed. They said something to each other that I did not hear and laughed again. Then one of them went a little closer to Abbas. Just fuck off, mate. And leave the vicar alone. The soldier raised his rifle butt. Abbas pointed at me. His fury made him brave. You bastard bloody bastard Scotch prick! I suppose he had learned such vile expressions off a sailor. Or a parrot. The soldiers snickered. One pressed the end of his rifle into Abbas's paunch. Don't push your luck, mate. Just fuck off. Sullenly Abbas climbed back into his Rolls Royce. As he drove off one of the soldiers took aim. For an awful moment I thought he was shooting at Abbas to kill him but it transpired he was simply engaged in a spot of fun. With impressive skill he hit both rear tyres. Each ring of inflated rubber exploded with a noise equal to that of the rifle shot which had caused it. The Rolls swerved from side to side, then came to a stop. Abbas sprang out and examined the damage. He shook his fist and screamed another stream of incomprehensible Arabic. Then he climbed back in and drove off, wobbling drunkenly from side to side. And that was the last I ever saw of the abominable Abbas, as he manoeuvred his erratic machine to the end of the street and out of my sight. In my book I shall say nothing of this. In my book there will be a touching scene in which Abbas sinks to his knees, hands clasped as if in prayer, and thanks me for my astonishing generosity. We will part the best of friends. This is the kind of thing readers prefer and one must never disappoint the reader.

AND SO MY ADVENTURES in the Holy Land came to their end. In spite of all, on my last day in Jerusalem I was not stuck for something to do. I had one holy place left to cross off my list. The cave of Jeremiah, prophet of Jerusalem's doom. Jeremiah: old misery guts, with a clairvoyant gift! I do apologise. That was uncalled for. It's the heat. It makes me light-headed, facetious, foolish. I cannot always control myself. Of the whereabouts of this legendary cavern I had made enquiries. Perplexingly it turned out there were two, each asserting its authenticity and indignantly refuting the claims made by the other. This muddy debate need not concern you. Suffice it to say that Donald Ebenezer McCollum Ph.D is a man not easily fooled. I believe I have a modest gift for sniffing out truth from falsehood and I soon decided which of these two tenebrous nooks was the real one. My advisor gave me directions but these were, I discovered, not entirely accurate. Perhaps this is only to be expected when you take direction from an Arab. I can only say that for me the second on the left, then right, then right again did me no good at all. I became lost. However, if you shout loud enough you will eventually be understood, and thus it was. History had not been kind to St Jeremiah because it had allowed a Palestinian family to make their home under the hillock where he had found stony lodgings. The legendary quality of things was quite, quite ruined by the urban environs. Once this would have been a lonely place, now it was simply another seething warren of Arabs and their ramshackle dwellings. Above me loomed a bleak, bare mound from which protruded a solitary fruit-bearing fig tree and some clumps of thorny cactus. A pair of small dark hollows in its flanks resembled eye sockets. Was this miserable and marginalised place the true site of Golgotha? The thought made my head swim. Had no one noticed the resemblance before? Yet the Biblical feel was terribly spoiled. Shouts rang out from some metalworkers and their forge smeared the perspective with dirty smoke. Nevertheless one must make the best of things. I must confess it was something of a relief to see so many policemen and soldiers in the streets. Some were on patrol and searching displays of vegetables (for you can never really be sure that that wrinkled toothless old vendor is really all that he seems – under those oranges may lurk a frightful hand grenade!). Others had halted passing carts and were emptying their contents into the street. The Arabs shrieked like monkeys when this happened, though they soon quietened down when a rifle was pointed at them. Some of the troops and police simply stood on street corners, watching. I was pleasantly surprised when soldiers, observing my dog collar, gave me a respectful salute. When they did this I always smiled and nodded and said Bless you, my son. But I did not take matters further. I have never believed in pushing religion down anyone's throat and though the British soldier may be a good Christian he is also a busy man. Besides, God works in many ways, some of which – and here one must be quite frank about the price that sometimes has to be paid to maintain the civilising influence of empire – may require cartridges and a well-oiled rifle. The house was easy enough to find, because it had a wooden sign attached to it bearing the words JEREMIAH CAVE. I tried the wooden door set in a high white wall and it opened. Visitors had to pass down the side of a house. At the back I came to a table with a biscuit tin lid on it. Behind the table sat a girl who was perhaps fourteen. Her breasts seemed large for a child. Her English was unexpectedly good. She told me the cost of admission and pointed at the lid. I laid the required coins on the silver surface and she nodded and pointed to the end of the family garden. A dirt path led past a few withered olive trees to a grotto set in the side of the brown slope which rose up, almost vertical. At its base what might have been scatterings of *Bellis perennis*. Remembered, probably falsely, in scattered recollections of an unfortunate episode. Lumps of rock protruded from that crumbling edifice. I asked if there was a guide, she said no. Her father was the guide and he was absent. The family were all at a funeral. Blooder, she said. It took a minute or so to grasp that she meant her brother. The family had left her behind to look after Jeremiah's cave. I gazed at her eyes for signs of sorrow but saw none. She was inscrutable, yet eager to please. She tugged at my sleeve. This way to cave. I followed her down a rocky path, past some chickens. A tethered goat eyed me malevolently. The cave entrance was a narrow man-sized gash. The girl was carrying a saucer with a candle. She stepped into the darkness and a match flared. She led me on. Inside the darkness opened out. The grotto was surprisingly spacious. It rose to a height beyond the range of the girl's candle. The walls curved back, growing narrower as they went deeper into the hill. Their rough, chipped texture made me wonder if this had once been some sort of mine. There was a faint musty smell. Somewhere there was mould growing. Or perhaps it was me. I sometimes wondered about my European odour. No matter how often my clothes were laundered they always seemed to carry the scent of something faintly damp. The girl held the candle so that, crouching, I could see to the end. The cave shrank to the size of a rabbit hole, then terminated in rubble. Perhaps there was a way through. Had anyone excavated this place? I asked the girl but she did not seem to understand. I stood up, my legs tingling. The candlelight illuminated grey trails of dampness on the walls. The dampness here would have been congenial to the saint's lachrymose moods. I found it entirely plausible that Jeremiah had been here. The print marks on the sandy floor might have been recently made by his sandaled feet. Time slides in this Holy Land. A thousand years pass in a moment. Jesus is tangibly present, as though he died only last Tuesday. This place was far enough from the tumult of the old city yet near enough to the temple area to be the place. An old man, resting on a rock, one hand supporting his bearded chin. Here Jeremiah came, alone, despondent and angry. In those days he had no neighbours. From this darkness a man can truly understand those who have departed from God. *Cut off thy hair, O Jerusalem, and cast it off. Take up a lamentation on the bare heights, for Jehovah hath rejected and forsaken the generation of his wrath.* Here a man might weep in secret (my own eyes began to moisten). Here a man might shake with despair and his eyes run down with tears (I felt a pair of salt drops meander down my hot face). O remorseless bitter world! O faithless, treacherous, villainous, godless city! Who in such a condition would not find a comforting shelter in a stony wilderness as this? Yet in that dark I also saw a pair of eyes, the red eyes of the goat. Satan's eyes. A soft voice whispering. Wilt thou yet take all, Galilean? The time for self-restraint is past. Of the event itself I can say little. Time slid - slides by - darkly. And besides… What was it Benjamin Franklin said? Three may keep a secret if two of them are dead. The same goes for two and one. What memory there is of it dissolves like a handkerchief dipped in acid. It, to wit, the event. The occurrence. The episode. The memory was already crumbling before I was long quit of that cool place. She looked at me with big wondering eyes. It was because I was crying, I think. I took hold of the top of her jerkin. I wrenched the cloth apart. Her breasts plopped out like fruit. I stripped away the remaining vestments. I cannot pretend I have not frequently re-imagined what occurred. Filling a darkness with form, so to speak. Putting a pair of humans on that stony stage. A man, a child. I speak of the irruption of blind desire. It is disgusting. It disgusts me to think of it. It burst from a knowledge that what was about to occur was possible, better than possible, an event without consequences, sans punishment, an imperial ecstasy, hence all. All the greasy grappling, the savage blind rabid plunge of rancid desire, bestial brutish bald lust, the shuddering ecstasy, just adjectives, token words, I recall few of the particulars, unless through mist, shadow, a darkling curtain. Her private parts astonishingly hairy. My lust like a knife. A style drawn from reflection. How convenient you say, you'd be right I suppose. I recall much more vividly the aftermath. The girl did not resist my embraces. Perhaps she was disabled by a paralysis of surprise and bewilderment. But afterwards she cried. As I re-adjusted my flies she stared down at the sandy floor. She was sobbing. Her sobs grew louder. I was reminded – I cannot remember if then or later – of a salt wave dragging back down a steep shelf of Dorset shingle. All I recall is that gulping loudness. We had both lost something, yet my own loss was framed by a hot cunning. That noise had to be stopped. It might produce consequences. *Death and life are in the power of the tongue: and they that love it shall eat the fruit thereof.* At first I was very nice. Please stop that noise I said, stop that do you hear, she didn't, be quiet I said, again a little more forcefully: be quiet. Listen, just bloody shut up! One thing leads to another – what awfulness boils below the surface of that banal truth. I recall none of the particulars. Nor do I profess to follow the teachings of Christ as they are conventionally rendered. I find no compatibility with my circumstances. Hands have no memory of the past. Mine did what they did, no more, no less. They squeezed. My verbal appeals having failed – the girl's upset was becoming distinctly strident – my grip around her throat tightened. She still wouldn't stop her racket. Further pressure was applied and her head of a sudden lolled forward. Her body became loose, into the house with it. Do you people know how heavy a dead child is? Of course you don't. Oh my materialistic brethren, trapped in your petty lives, numbing yourselves with gin and horse-racing and whist. You who abuse yourselves with Hollywoodenonanism. You who are betrayed not by Judas but by Rita Hayworth. How could you know about such weights? I got the girl inside. I put it down on the floor, the body. I distinctly remember tiles, orange tiles. I left matters there and went for a wander in my own private wilderness. The Lord was with me, this I know. I do not pretend to understand the workings of He Who Is All-Knowing, but I do know that He was behind everything I did that day. Mine was to be the thorny path to salvation. Sin is behovely if it brings us unto Thee. I drifted from room to room. I was the ghost of my former self. I had gone over the border and was now another. A fly – a fat nauseating bluebottle – appeared and started pestering me. I lashed out, driving it away. It returned, like Satan. I slapped at it with my guilty right hand. In the end it flew out of a window and left me in peace. I sat down to get my breath back. I lay down on a bed and dozed off. A screaming like a gull's woke me, I have no idea what it was. I was wild that day. I had gone across into a new world, at night. There was a lurid light at the edge of everything, shimmering. I rocked and reeled with laughter, I gurgled with amusement, what came over me I do not know. I found myself in another bedroom, a double bed with a bright coverlet, patterned, scarlet and blue. The parental arbour, I presume. I felt loose, at liberty to do whatever I wanted, this was an infidel household was it not? There are many devices in a man's heart. I wanted to smash up everything but it was hot and I was tired. I contented myself with a few pots. I tipped them on to the hard floor and smiled as they shattered. A better idea. All those ingots stacked up inside my bowels, all those pellets of waste matter compressed by my constipated system, were in a trice turned molten. The bricks and plugs were melted into slush. My guts were boiling. I pull back the covering and empty myself on the sheet, a huge splattering yellow-brown sloppy mess. I neatly put the coverlet back, a surprise! Next I wipe myself on the edge of the sheet, tuck it neatly in (another surprise!). Downstairs I came across an axe. I dragged the body to another bedroom and went back for my tool. Why I dismembered the body I cannot really say. A holy madness was inside me that incandescent morning. I could hear a clock ticking. It was as loud as the chimes of Big Ben. Time's loud, coarse passage did not concern me. In retrospect the risks I took were dizzying. Had the family returned and discovered me I dread to think what might have happened. The Arab is a creature of wild impulses. I suspect I would have been martyred for my faith. There was a low cunning inside me, I suppose. I had the wit to strip off all my clothes before I began my butcher's task. I left a neat pile just outside the room. I did not wish to get anything splashed. Back with the corpse I was startled to find myself once more in a state of tumescence. You will be delighted to learn I did not add necrophilia to my sins. Instead I got to work. I hacked madly until there were two portions. The slicing seemed to go on for many minutes, splish-splash-splatter, I shall spare you what you are free to imagine. Intestines unfold to remarkable lengths. They are not a pretty sight. And now it's all gone, a moth-eaten purple curtain shuts out the scene, an adjective and a noun are a sufficient shield. I could play the novelist and pretend all this is just a cheap dream, I shan't. I was right to take precautions. By the end, I was quite bespattered. I found a room with water and cleansed myself. Then I towelled myself dry and dressed. I have no memory of this but I must have done so. And so on with the story. Another bright idea! Downstairs there is a room set aside for prayer and worship. My bladder aches and where better? Afterwards the air is salt and stinging with the odour of my Christianity. The Lord fuels my contempt for heresy. The yellow jet seems to go on forever before finally stopping. Next I take the big Koran down and start to rip out clumps of pages, they mean nothing to me, just squiggles and scimitars, filthy black markings, a declaration of war. My trusty Swan Vestas will not let me down, this is holy work. The crackling begins. Can you believe the oddest thing of all? There, at the end of this greasy little episode, excitement and desire rose up like a weary victor's flagpole on a ruinous battlefield. I yet again did some unbuttoning and kneeled. I spat on my palms and attended to this unexpected demand. My seed shot like soft bullets into the fire. How the pages of the Koran hissed in anger at the presence of a fertile Christian! There is a sweet parable in all this, surely. For this barren land is being reclaimed for Zion and the honeyed seed of the righteous. And the unproductive shall be driven out, along with their dark superstitions and idolatry. Looked at rationally, could there be a greater absurdity than Mohammedanism? I left the house with a roaring in my ears. My blood, or arson's breed, I cannot say. I could hear the Lord's wrath against that house, the multiplying tongues of fire, they sang in my head like a choir. Flame curling catlike around the bright cushions on the floor. The roar of a throbbing conscience, of course not, delete that sentimental addition. I am trying to be straight with myself. I reached the front door, unbolted it. It did not occur to me to go back round the side of the house. Behind me the spitting and gushing grew in intensity, a tide of boiling lava meeting a mighty waterfall, enough of this drivel. I stepped out into the street and shut the door quickly behind me. It was noisier out than in, the screech of a camel, a braying donkey, a caterwauling street vendor with strips of spicy chicken. I flinched at the Lord's harsh noontime gaze. He fixed me with His celestial attention but said nothing. I sensed His unwillingness to make a snap judgement. Repentance and prayers might well fix it for me. My punishment for now is sunlight, tightly focused on my scarlet dripping face. The police saw me at once. So did the soldiers. They were just the other side of the street in two groups, chatting. They stiffened as I stepped out, I saw their hands go for their guns. They were fearful of an ambush. And then they relaxed at the sight of a member of the civilised races. *One of us.* A pink-faced chubby cherub wearing a Panama hat. I beamed back and tipped it respectfully. A stir of recognition among one of the soldiers, a Lance Corporal Somebody, one of Orde's assistants possibly, I cannot be certain. I continued to nod and smile but did not communicate my usual blessing. They started to lose interest, went back to their chit-chat. My head continued to be filled with a terrible din. Flee from the wrath to come! Angels contended with devils. A remembered moment from *Macbeth* was hurriedly staged and then the theatre filled with smoke and the audience began to scream. I remembered to saunter. I pottered, sweating copiously, to the end of the street. A thudding boiling heart shook the neighbourhood, unnoticed. I was waiting for the mob to point at me, to identify me as the criminal, to seize me. I was waiting for the accusing shouts, the furious screams, the cries of fire! None came. Perhaps I had botched things. The fire had fizzled and gone out. No matter. Soon the family would be back. But by then I would be gone. The day went on like any other Jerusalem day. The barter of commodities under a blue sky. I took the first available alleyway, and then another. I broke out into a street, crossed it, and found new alleyways. Jerusalem was full of dead flesh that day. Chickens with broken necks on hooks. A fluffy dangling lamb with its throat cut. Lumps of dark dripping meat on racks alive with clouds of flies. A smiling proprietor with a flit gun. On. The fruit market, the spice market, the bazaar of the metal workers. On down the Via Dolorosa. A lurching camel passes, shaking its tasselled head. Some calm sweet-tempered overloaded donkeys. Female beggars, their veils black and white. Loud tourists with Kodaks and yelping American voices. A procession of miserable-looking English Christians, in clothes the colour of mud or mould, advancing slowly over the creamy flagstones. Solemn ponderous Ashkenezim Jews with enormous black hats edged with grey fur. The Greek quarter, coffin lids of ebony displayed by the doors of undertakers. Small shops suffused with the smell of incense, selling olive wood camels. A bell tolling, then more bells, the whole city at last jangling and clanging with sundry iron reverberations until I felt like screaming. My head throbbed and ached terribly. A bronze plate reading in smaller letters, after some Hebrew, JEWISH AGENCY. I dash inside and run up the stairs. I enter an office which is a hive of activity. It reminded me of a newspaper office in a Hollywood film. The place was full of desks and young men and women furiously typing. People standing around in groups were chattering in all the languages of the civilised nations. I could hear Spanish, German and French. There was some jabber which might well have been Russian. The speaker looked like Trotsky, with a wispy beard and owl-eyes glasses. On the walls were many maps to which pins had been stuck. Can I help you? My inquisitor was cold, ferocious and filled with suspicion. He looked to be about forty. With that nose of his he reminded me of a falcon. I could not help but note that he had a pistol tucked into his belt. I am an enormous admirer of your enterprise, I said. I have come from Scotland. My father, the Lord bless him, brought me up to admire the dream which you people are making real. I am a church minister, but lately come from a motor tour of the holy sites. I regret to say that at the end I had an unfortunate experience with my Arab chauffeur. But I know I can tell you nothing about the fecklessness of aboriginals that you yourselves do not already know. I have seen with my own eyes how you are making the desert bloom. I have here a modest donation. Please spend it as you think best. I took out my wallet and handed over twenty pounds. What unending wildness was in me that day! But what use is twenty pounds to a man who is to be hanged? The fellow grunted and took the bank notes. I regret to say he did not display the effusive gratitude which I was rather expecting. But no matter. The Jew can be a strange creature at times. I hurried back down the stairwell. From here, wherever that was, I took a taxi back to my hotel.

EDITH WAS HER name. As we crossed Gaza and Palestine slipped away I asked her to marry me. She said yes at once and we lived happily ever after. Our homely home in the Hebrides rings with the laughter of our three darling children, and as I step across the threshold I can smell the delicious aroma of home-cooking – oatcakes, bubbling porridge and the stench of black pudding. Believe that and you'll believe anything. It might have happened like that, of course. But it did not. That said, Edith is the only woman who has ever made me consider that sexual intercourse on a regular basis might be a procedure somewhat less than repellent. I finished my packing and checked out of the King David Hotel. After various wearisome complications and undiverting diversions I ended up on the Kantara train. My carriage was empty apart from a delightful English girl. She had rosy cheeks and a band of freckles across her nose. Her tousled hair was a rich, deep auburn. She smelled of violets. (As you can tell I am still half in love with easeful Edith.) At first we were a little shy of each other and maintained our reserve. Her merry blue eyes were directed at the view rather than yours truly. But then sunlight filled the space between us and suddenly we both simultaneously remarked on the glorious palm oases on the marge of each perfect beach. We broke into laughter as they do in films and soon we were exchanging stories. Her blue pleated skirt had ridden up her legs. I caught a glimpse of a suspender strap. Her stockings were the colour of sand. Her thighs were deliciously plump. Edith explained she had flown up from Cairo to visit her air-force brother at Lydda Landing Field. I told her a little about myself and my pilgrimage to those very special places in the Holy Land. Our blue smiling steam train chugged merrily among lovely sand dunes close by the azure Mediterranean. The sand here is herring-boned with exquisite wind-carved patterns. From time to time we glimpsed lines of white camels, driven by winged men in floating veils. It seemed magical. But then we came to the mud huts of old Gaza, still unrepaired after Allenby's ancient fight with the Turks. I told Edith of the remarkable history of the region and of the marvellous work of Sir Flinders Petrie. She gasped as I told her how this admirable old fellow – still hard at work at the age of eighty-three! – had excavated gold jewellery from Ireland here, in the mount of ancient Ghazzeh, named Tel el-'Aijul. I may have babbled, I admit. Edith was a nervy girl, and nervy girls give me the jitters. Her laughter was unnatural.

It had a slightly forced quality. She seemed to laugh at everything, yet I sensed an underlying disgust. Something was troubling her. My condition was no better. I maintained an observation of sand and sea and whatever chose to fill those vacant spaces but all the time I was waiting for the train to grind to an unexpected halt and the police to come on board. They would move from carriage to carriage, searching for a murderer. It would be like *The 39 Steps*, with me as Robert Donat. But I knew I would not jump off. It was too late for all that. There would be nowhere to hide in this bare landscape, and besides I am not awfully energetic. Running at speed is not my cup of tea. Fear made me voluble. I rather think I may have blathered. But Edith was a good egg and did not try to shut me up. She freely admitted her Bible illiteracy and listened with interest as I told her about Emmaus and about the border-country through which our train was speeding. Edith, a sharp girl, observed that no one was swimming. She thought it was such a waste of these beautiful sandy beaches. I quipped that it was *the Philistine Riviera* and Edith flashed her almost perfect teeth and broke into peals of laughter at my wit. I must confess I found the amusement of a pretty girl a distinctly pleasurable experience. I wanted to get out my Kodak and photograph her. Something I could look at for the rest of my life. But I lacked the courage. Instead I stared out of the carriage window. I was becoming aware of its faint scratch marks and semen-coloured stains. Deserted beaches gave way to villages. That is the Arab for you, I said, solemnly pointing at the dusky-hued families huddled in the shade of mud and grass huts. They are only interested in their plantations. We stared at the hedged rectangles of land, full of corn and melon and bananas, but soon grew bored. More and more desert sand blew in through the open window, a fine mist that bid fair to bury us like the Sphinx. With our powdered hair and clothing we resembled a pair of corpses, determined to continue talking in spite of adversity. It was strangely peaceful in that carriage, where leather straps gently tapped the walnut panels and the creep of a dying afternoon led us towards a mauve ending. By now we were practically chums and Edith opened up about the true state of affairs. She had really come to Palestine to think things over. An army Padre had asked her to marry him. She wasn't sure and needed time to think. She thought she'd make a pretty poor parson's wife. She liked dancing and films and having fun. Gerald – her Padre – couldn't dance for toffee. And have you come to a decision? I felt my heart thudding as I put the question. Edith laughed gaily and shrugged. I don't know, she said. I just don't know. Then marry me instead. She gawped. *You!* I've got quite a decent income, I said. When my father dies I shall inherit a tidy sum. And I own a house that's far too big for a bachelor. Where is it? Stornoway, I said. Well strictly speaking not in Stornoway but in that neck of the woods. You wouldn't have heard of it. Where's Stornoway? The Hebrides. The Hebrides? She roared with laughter. That's in Scotland, isn't it? Yes it is, I conceded. I could never live in Scotland, she said. It rains all the time there. And there are millions of midges. I once had a camping holiday north of Glasgow. I *hate* midges. I positively *loathe* them. So I shall have to decline. But it's awfully sweet of you to ask. I've decided it will have to be Gerald. Her words disgusted me. I cried: But you just said you weren't sure! She grinned, obscenely buoyant. Oh but I am now. You've helped me make up my mind. Look, do you know how old I jolly well am? I hazarded a guess. Twenty-five? That's awfully sweet of you to say so. But the fact is I'm thirty. But don't for Lord's sake tell Gerald if you ever meet him, because he thinks I'm twenty-seven. And frankly my chances of getting hitched are fading fast. That's not true, I said hotly. Take me, for instance. I could do with a wife. Very much so, in fact. I'm sure we could make a go of it. Lewis isn't so bad, you know. Who's Louis? I mean the island. Where I live, I said. Oh I could never live on an island, she said. I'd suffocate. But Britain's an island! That's different, she said. Anyway *I could do with a wife* isn't the most romantic proposal I've ever had. Not that it matters now. My heart was broken five years ago. A chap named Tom. As a matter of fact I gave myself to him. I can see that shocks you. Don't look so tragic. It was no sooner done than the poor fool crashed his plane and died. He was a pilot, you see. A friend of my brother's. But that's all water under the bridge. As I see it there's no point in crying over spilt milk. I'll make do and mend. That's what people do, isn't it? They just go on living as best they can, making the best of things. And Gerald might be a parson but at least he's army. All my family married army and I will too. Oh look! We've reached Suez.

AT THE BORDER settlement of Ishmailia the huge red sun of Egypt drops into the desert behind a rim of palms. A violet soft sensuous liquid twilight envelops us here. The blue night sky fills with a sparkling silver fire. It was once gazed at by tiny languorous Cleopatra on her couch. It must surely have solaced even desolate Hagar and Ishmael. I said to myself, remembering one of father's pamphlets, The End Times are here! At Cairo, at night, with my old pump thumping, I gave Edith an Egyptian farewell. Farewell, remember me. Three hand clasps, and three times our hands pressed against our beating hearts. I proffered my card but Edith shook her head and said she really didn't think she should take it. The future dropped like a vase and shattered. She kissed me on the cheek and grinned and called me an odd fish. Then she was gone. Her scent lingered in that carriage. That sweet chamber was suddenly as empty as a ransacked tomb. I saw her one more time, on the seething, crowded concourse. She pushed her way through the crowds to a man in khaki. Gerald was bigger than I'd imagined. His face was radish-bright and fleshy. He reminded me of an inert crustacean. The creature spasmed into life. It hugged Edith and then applied saliva to her mouth and face. Sick with misery and disgust I turned away. A taxi took me through the raucous animated night streets to the Imperial Hotel, where the city's noise was hushed and I slept like an opium fiend. In the morning I ate a hearty breakfast and drank three stinging peppery cups of coffee. I had planned four more days in Cairo, before joining a ship at Port Said. There was still a spot of sightseeing to pack in. I wondered if I had the courage to include a brothel. I felt wild and lewd and furious. Edith seemed to taunt me with her boiling absence. I was in the mood to soil something. But it was not to be. I was back in my room staring at a map when there was a knock at the door. Two policemen stood there. Their faces were grim. There were pistols strapped to their hips. I knew what it was about, obviously. I'd been a fool to think it could end any other way. Orde's man had spotted me the moment I'd stepped out of that burning house. Identification of the murderer hardly required the deductive genius of Mr Sherlock Holmes. It was little more than a bureaucratic formality. A paper trail of hotel registrations, train reservations and border controls led to killer. You had better come in, I said. I suppose. Or perhaps the senior policeman said: May we come inside? And I replied: Yes, of course. I remember so little of past conversations. I am always surprised when people write their autobiographies and remember the things they said and others said forty years before. I struggle to recall what I said yesterday, or even this morning. Whatever was said, I held back the door and they stepped inside. I closed the door. The officers were wearing short trousers and long grey socks, giving them the appearance of schoolboys. The one in charge had a toothbrush moustache, like the Fuehrer. Would you like a drink? I said. I was playing for time. A tumbler of whisky and a few more minutes of freedom before the handcuffs put in an inevitable appearance. Hitler smiled bleakly. Normally we wouldn't drink on duty, he said. But on this occasion… This can't be easy for you, I said. I have no idea why I said that. Call it another of my light-hearted caprices. Probably it was something I had once read in a crime novel. I have a keen sense of the proprieties and the conventions. Their consent to alcohol startled me, just as my words seemed to startle them. I added: Would you like me to make a statement? I am happy to co-operate in any way possible. I don't wish to be difficult. The officers frowned. I was aware that once again my natural urge to loquacity had manifested itself. I shut up. I poured the drinks. They raised no objection to Johnny Walker. I passed them their refreshment. Down the hatch! Down the hatch, they echoed. No statement will be necessary, Dr McCollum. In fact by the sound of it you may have got the wrong end of the stick. I regret to inform you I have some bad news, doctor. This phrasing did not seem quite right for rape, murder, mutilation and arson. Had I been barking up the wrong tree all the time? Indeed I had. Although I cannot pretend that the fellow's next words were any less terrible than an announcement that I was under arrest on suspicion of monstrous crimes. Hitler drained his glass and looked at me. The fact is we have some rather bad news. I regret to inform you that your father is seriously ill. He has asked to see you. I'm afraid the message has taken some time to reach you. Apparently it was passed on to your hotel in Jerusalem after you'd left. It took some time to work out where you were. But not to worry, now that we've tracked you down everything is under control. The chaps at the embassy have managed to book you on a plane leaving this afternoon. I have brought you the ticket. I'm afraid you'll have to reimburse HM Government. But no need to worry about that now. The main thing is to get you home. Would you like me to get the hotel to order you a taxi? You'll need to leave by three at the latest. Shall we say two-thirty? Two-thirty would be quite suitable, I said. My voice felt weak and shaky. In truth my feelings were a harsh combination of distress at the news of my poor father's illness – it was obvious reading between the lines that he was dying – and a fierce elation that my crimes had not yet caught up with me. If I managed to get out of Egypt before the day was over then probably they never would. No one could drag me back to Palestine to answer questions. The law, I was fairly certain, would not permit it. I had read something to that effect in one of the newspapers. After the officers had gone I began re-packing my only recently unpacked belongings. Interrupted only by a sudden boiling in my bowels. I ran to the lavatory. My anus squirted a foul yellow jet. Shit like watery custard, stinking to high heaven. In a word: diarrhoea. A gyppy tummy. I wiped myself clean and then was caught in the grip of another cascade. The squares of Izal ran out. Luckily a fellow Briton had left two copies of the *Times Literary Supplement* on a ledge beside the water closet. Each page folded in half, then torn, makes for a luxury arse wipe. It was a shame I'd had no time to read the reviews but *c'est la vie*. Two copies sufficed to return me to the land of sweetness and hygiene. My voiding was done with. I ate bread, in the firm belief that this keeps you in a condition of solidity and control. It seemed to work for me. Which brings me on to last things.

THERE IS NO ending in life, other than the brute and obvious one. With stories it's different. A lot of things accumulate and go on accumulating. There are weights, pressures. Where to stop? Where to begin? A man can easily become abject and look for an easy way out. You can over-simplify. You can flannel and blather and not mention the unmentionable. Best not to mention the unmentionable, really. People won't like you for it. I could end this story at Croydon Airport, in the rain. This was where I learned that I was too late. My father had died during the flight. You might say he died in my sleep, if I slept, I can't be sure. I like to think I did. Father dead. The revelation left me unmoved. I calmly thanked the bearer. No tears would come then, or later. My father's wealth was a lot less than he had led me to believe. The tears on my face at his graveside were splashes of rain from bruise-dark louring cumulus. I adopted the style that was expected of me under those grave conditions. My heart was dry and without turbulence. None of this seems to matter. I hope as a prelude to my own interment someone will salute not only a devout theologian but a man with a sly sense of humour. A returned prince might well recall my pranks. Back at the house I discovered a granule from the cave lodged between two of my toes. The skin was raw and pink where it had rubbed abrasively. I doubt if the dull-witted police would ever have discovered it, even if I had been incarcerated in Cairo. But all that was far behind me by then. Wet days turned to cold weeks, the wintry weeks to months of Mondayish moods. And then I put off my sackcloth. I girded me with gladness. God be merciful to me, a sinner. I repent now of all my sins and turn from them. I place my trust alone in the Lord Jesus Christ for Salvation. I believe that the Blood of Jesus shed for me on the Cross atones for my sins. I now accept the finished work of Christ. The book was written and published and reviewed. It sold, though far fewer copies than the publishers expected. The market for travel books collapsed once the war broke out. The war spoiled so many things. In point of fact I rather regret the way things have panned out. Hitler, it seems to me, is not as black as he has been painted in some quarters. Everyone seems to forget that a rapprochement was agreed with the German Zionist Federation. A sensible and civilised agreement was reached that all German Jews could be assisted to start a new life in a homeland for the Jews, to wit in Palestine. This was why the Zionist Federation deplored the irresponsible attempts by the fanatics of the Left to campaign for a boycott of German goods. Indeed, one of Wingate's pals told me that the warmest of links had been forged. It was only a few years ago that a correspondent of *Der Angriff* was invited out to see for himself how the answer to the so-called 'Jewish question' was laid out for all to see in this dusty strip of the globe, where a people prepared to get stuck in and work hard will one day create one of the more civilised and humane states on this little spinning globe of ours. Wingy's chum (who had been involved with the organisation) even had a souvenir of the visit – a collection of yellowing newspaper cuttings entitled *A Nazi Visits Palestine*. He also proudly showed me his commemorative medallion, with the Star of David on one side and the swastika on the other. When people tell you that Joseph Goebbels is anti-Semitic I beg you to remember that. Speaking as one doctor about another I have always rather admired the fellow. His facial features may have the misfortune to resemble those of a syphilitic skull, yet his tastes have, from what little I have learned, always been civilised. And not everything in war turns out badly. Swings and roundabouts, eh? For all I know the war may have helped my own fortunes, obscurely. For no inspector ever came to call. No writ of hocus-pocus was ever drawn up against me. Amid so much death, I am very small fry. I was – I am! - a scot-free Scot. Make me a new creation in Christ Jesus and give me power in my life to live for Thee and serve Thee. Where no wood is, there the fire goeth out: so where there is no tale-bearer, the strife ceaseth. Autumn crept in like a reptile. Its bone structure could not be disguised. Granite winked at me. My hands turn into claws. An old fever returns. Outside, the distant plugs and tumours of volcanic outpourings sweat off their centuries of rain. A pretty enough sight. I could spin this story out if I wanted to. The further I went, the more I would relish it. Things unbelievable! In the meantime, mean time lets slide its lava. I shall drown in it. It petrifies me. They'll find me solidified, bent over in a last desperate lurch for shelter. I am no Flavius Claudius Julianus. So no sarcophagus of porphyry for poor old Donald McCollum. Anything else that the defendant would like to say? Lord, yes. Year after year passes and I still think of Edith, out there somewhere. Perhaps she is still in Egypt. I think of this war, soon to be over. Back in the Hebrides I went back to my old ways. With father gone I was free to lubricate my life in any vile way I wished. Whisky and butter and spittle were the wines which irrigated my dark obscure wound. Sometimes, at 3 a.m., I rise (already risen!) in my empty house. I go outside, into the garden. The pale night shows the ragged outline of the mountains. The world has grown grey from His breath. I slip off my striped pyjamas by the back door. What happens next is anyone's guess. Correction. *How* what happens next is anyone's guess. The outcome itself is never in doubt. The thing itself comes to a sticky conclusion. Conscience, guilt, disgust, they each combine to yap at my naked self. Lust drives them off with a big stick. No gastrorrhaphy can ever seal my aching, throbbing flesh. Sometimes, when in a daredevilish mood, I take a wild risk. I haul myself up one of Nora's old cast iron poles. I balance there, purple trigger pressed against the cold, coarse surface. Above me, the twinkling stars and rags of speeding cloud. I hang there, shuddering, until at last I lower myself back on to the surface of this bitter planet. But mostly I prefer not to take chances. I make my way to where no intruding stranger can ever see me. I crouch stark amid the shrubs. I push myself backward against spiky branches, sometimes even to the point of tearing open skin. Such little drips of hot blood excite me no end. Algolagnia is sweeter than honey. My fury pierces the night. I boil with longings. I have carnal knowledge of – oh wicked, wicked – the Holy Trinity itself. Trembling, shuddering, teeth-clenched, I splash the cold damp grass with my milk. A low, crawling ghost mauls the withered mulberry bush. It chills my calves. I fart in God's face. I stand above the rose bush and piss upon its blossom. I return indoors, bloated with shame and fear. I go back to bed and cannot sleep. I am back at Cairo airport now, the propellers whirling, the fuselage trembling, the din of the engine unbelievably loud. A dentist's cruel drill, burrowing deeper into my skull. Take-off in three minutes. The steps have been removed. They can't get me now. The motive for my passage is at this point absent from my mind. I cannot think of a dying father at a time like this. The great machine taxis across the runway. Power and force roll me with them, their humble priest. The horizon has a greenish-amber hue. The first stars are coming out. We howl up the runway. With a savage sliding lurch the aircraft frees itself from the pull of hot, earthly things. Steeply upward we continue on life's journey. Goodbye old slithery black snake Nile! The fluffy cloud layer slips past. We level off. Hell and damnation! A tiny prick of pain in one of my feet, it's nothing. Would like to get some sleep but sleep won't come. I keep my eyes closed tight. That's what father always said I should do to ensure a good night's sleep. Doesn't seem to work on a plane. No real sleep. Was that what Satan promised me a long, long time ago? Nonsense and stuff! Keep trying. Must always keep at it. Tighter, tighter. Empty my boiling mind. Let it all pour away, the silt, the muck. Shut down the damned choir. Close the lid on the organ. Complete inertia and silence, *please.* I hear a child, sobbing. I try my very best to shut her out. Please give me a drink. Please send me assorted literature. Silence, do you hear! Impossible on a plane. But once we've levelled off the engine din diminishes, markedly. The whirr of the propellers is strangely soothing. Please send me a helpful Christian book. Please send me Further Spiritual Help. For I hear a crying in the dark core of screaming machinery. There's a wailing inside the shivering fuselage. It pierces my continuing fever. A worm wriggles inside the cushion under my head. Go away! Give me some peace. Let me relax and enjoy the view. We are on course for England's green fields. Up here everything is a rich dark beauteous imperial blue. The darkling heavens seem lively with God's shining presence. I feel Him in my blood. I sense His mercy. O Lord my God, I will give thanks to Thee forever. And then again I hear return the tongues of all the wronged.

New York Times Book Review (August 1939)

The reader can open this volume assured that he will find here something very different to the usual book on Palestine. Dr McCollum has been inspired by a great number and variety of interests, historical, social, and economic but above all spiritual.

The book describes the author's adventures as he goes in search of the life of Christ and the landscape which saw the birth of Christianity. Dr McCollum is the son of a minister in the Church of Scotland, a man who, as he puts it, 'first set my moral compass in the direction of virtue.' He movingly describes how his tour of Palestine served only to revivify his faith. But this is no dusty tract. The author has jogged around, up and down, all over Palestine in an old motor car driven by a picturesque and amusing Arab chauffeur.

Intermingled with all of the varied threads of the narrative there runs a constant accompaniment of colorful description and comment that picture the daily scene and the persons that fill it. With the greatest zest, Dr McCollum describes the still discoverable trail of the Phoenicians, the excavations of the archaeologists and the inspiring work of those, many of them Americans, who are founding the new homeland of Zion and bringing this backward region into the modern world.

The author describes the many new friends he found there, including loyal servants of the Mandate who are selflessly toiling to bring peace and civilisation to a region where dark and ignorant forces sometimes seek to obstruct the forward march of progress.

A Jaunt through Palestine is as informing, interesting and engaging a book on its theme as one is likely to find.

It ought to be particularly useful for anyone taking the increasingly popular cruise into Eastern Mediterranean waters.